featherless

featherless

a novel

a.g. mojtabai

SL/.NT
BOOKS

FEATHERLESS
A Novel

Copyright © 2024 A.G. Mojtabai. All rights reserved. Except for brief quotations in critical publications or reviews, no part of this book may be reproduced in any manner without prior written permission from the publisher. Write: Permissions, Slant Books, P.O. Box 60295, Seattle, WA 98160.

Slant Books
P.O. Box 60295
Seattle, WA 98160

www.slantbooks.org

Cataloguing-in-Publication data:

Names: Mojtabai, A.G.
Title: Featherless: a novel / A.G. Mojtabai.
Description: Seattle, WA: Slant Books, 2024
Identifiers: ISBN 978-1-63982-178-5 (hardcover) | ISBN 978-1-63982-177-8 (paperback) | ISBN 978-1-63982-179-2 (ebook)
Subjects: LCSH: Old age--Fiction | Older people--Fiction | Nursing homes--Fiction | Nursing home residents--Fiction

To my daughter Chitra F. Mojtabai:
You collaborated with me on every page of this manuscript.
You bled over each and every word as much as I did.
Without you, *Featherless* would never have taken flight.
This book is half yours.

I dedicate this book to the wise and kind women who
have been my caregivers. I have learned so much from you.
Thank you for your attention and friendship, your patience
and compassion. Here's to my Texas Toughies: Lisa Tucek,
Pandora Box, Kimberley "Kiki" Grantham,
Tammie Whitley, and Anna Oritz.

And to Ramin Mojtabai and Masoumeh Amin-Esmaeil:
Long may you two reign.

A.G. (Grace) Mojtabai
October 7, 2024
Amarillo, Texas

In the end, only a small number of all this great company arrived at that sublime place to which the hoopoe had led them. Of the thousands of birds almost all had disappeared. Many had been lost in the ocean, others had perished on the summits of the high mountains, tortured by thirst; others had their wings burnt and their hearts dried up by the fire of the sun; others were devoured by tigers and panthers; others died of fatigue in the deserts and in the wilderness, their lips parched and their bodies overcome by the heat; some went mad and killed each other for a grain of barley; others, enfeebled by suffering and weariness, dropped on the road unable to go further; others, bewildered by the things they saw, stopped where they were, stupefied; and many, who had started out from curiosity or pleasure, perished without an idea of what they set out to find.

So then, out of all those thousands of birds, only thirty reached the end of the journey. And even these were bewildered, weary and dejected, with neither feathers nor wings.

—Farid Ud-Din Attar
The Conference of the Birds
Translated by Garcin
de Tassy and C.S. Nott

I

I

Birds on a Branch

FIVE—two men, three women, on a bench—
    Five birds on a branch overhead—
    Five featherless bipeds perched on a bench—
    A moment of perfect synchrony.
    One lifts off—
    Now there are four.

2

Daniel: Waking Late

THE PHONE was ringing—a gnat in his ear. The night before Daniel had thrown himself on the bed fully dressed (shoelaces too much of a bother to unlace). So when the phone began to ring, he pressed his face deep down into the pillow. When that failed to blot out the sound, he burrowed deeper. It was quieter there. Now he was running in his dream, only waking a half-second before crashing into the pavement. His heart lurched and skipped.

His eyes opened to full light. The phone was ringing. Had it been ringing all night?

"Where are you?"

Who asked that?

He burrowed once more and waited until the words became a mere fizzing in his ear.

But the phone wouldn't stop ringing.

Daniel: Waking Late

Daniel was rushing, almost running. He had been summoned to the Deputy Director's office. By now, he had worked out all the shortcuts on the route there.

This must be important. Passing the Restricted Access sign, Daniel felt important. He took the stairs two at a time.

But the Deputy Director was displeased.

He was a man of moods, and Daniel had read this wrong.

"Do you realize how hard we worked to get you situated? You're one lucky boy! Your rent and meals are taken care of! And you receive a salary! You can walk to work! We've been calling you since 5:00 a.m.!"

True enough: Daniel did and did not want to be reached. He had reason to be wary. It felt too easy to fall into other people's plans for him. He was uncomfortable with the word "situated," one of the Deputy Director's favorites. It did not fit his case, as he saw it. "Perched" would be more accurate but nothing so permanent as being "situated."

Often, Daniel would summarize his situation as "betwixt and between." Literally. His apartment had two windows: one overlooking Brewster Municipal Park and its playground and the other one facing the entrance to the Residence at Shady Rest, Home for the Aged, where he worked ten hours a day. He feared that his entire life might be already mapped along these two coordinates, that he could too easily be "situated" here, unable to leave—on call forever. Daniel thought of this job as a placeholder, nothing he had ever considered as a career. It had more or less been dropped in his lap—and proved a godsend in that respect—but it wasn't anything that would have occurred to him to go out of his way to apply for.

Peeved as he was, the Deputy Director had an assignment for him:

"We need you to handle something, Daniel. We need to nip this thing in the bud. PR needs to do some damage control."

The present issue was this: the night before, the emergency alarm had sounded at 4:21 a.m. Daniel had failed to hear it (or had he?). As he was now informed, the backstory behind management's urgent call stemmed from an incident that took place some years back. There had been a middle-of-the-night escape attempt by two love-stricken residents. They had been promptly collected and safely returned, but the former director, welcoming the friendly attentions of the press, made free use of the word "elopement" (an old-fashioned word rarely used these days, a euphemism covering prison breaks and runaway weddings alike). He had imagined the romantic version of their story might be a boon for recruitment and worked to keep it in the local news. That had been a mistake. He was promptly sacked, the event was not to be mentioned, and the present state-of-the-art alarm system had been installed. There had been no breaches since, until the night before. This time, it had been an actual elopement at the hopeful outset, but the fugitives who were fetched back that morning had been confused and shivering in their robes and slippers. That wouldn't be good publicity.

Daniel assured the Deputy Director that he would say what he had been told to say. That there was no security breach, merely a mechanical malfunction of the emergency back-up alarm system. (Although he was surprised that Shady Rest was that technologically prepared.) He found himself flattered again to be trusted with an administrative secret. Even if he didn't know what really happened.

Leaving the administrative offices, Daniel was disappointed to see that he was too late for breakfast. He'd been counting on having a few minutes over coffee to prepare for what would be his first unsupervised intake interview later that morning. Also, he was hungry.

As it happened, the old editor at the *Brewster Sentinel* had already heard about the 4:00 a.m. alarm and remembered the "elopement" story. He wanted to send someone out to see if there was something to it but didn't want to spare his top reporter. Instead, he would send out the new girl.

3

Brewster Sentinel Sends Out a Reporter

THAT MUST be Daniel.

The reporter had been told to look out for a young man named Daniel who would be attending to his usual group of residents.

She recognized him at a distance, shepherding his tiny flock.

He was not young. But not old.

The fresh face of a young man but with the slumped shoulders of a much older one—"neither fish nor fowl."

When they had settled themselves on their bench, she walked up and introduced herself as Amy Something from the *Brewster Sentinel*.

In the future, there would be much discussion about the reporter's last name. Daniel was sure he heard Leather, and Maddie remembered it as Feather. Eli insisted on Seller. Everyone heard something different, and for a while the subject became a reliable resource when conversation lagged. In the end, it didn't matter. They would not see her again.

Daniel introduced himself in turn, and the residents spoke their names: Eli, Gladys, Elora, and Maddie at the end of the bench.

Whether considered singly or together, Amy was unable to distinguish them one from the next. Their faces blurred and merged, all beiges and grays.

She had resolved not to grow old if she could help it. Still on the safe side of thirty with time yet—but not by much. Here it was, the twenty-first century, and they still hadn't figured it out. She had been reading a whole bunch of cutting-edge reports. These were real medical articles on Google. Double-blind studies. Calorie restriction to near starvation levels, slowing down the metabolism, or at the other extreme, an all-meat diet. Whatever it took. Brewster Community College was offering a night course called "Hibernation 101, Benefits and Risks." She had seriously considered auditing it.

Meanwhile, Daniel's recounting of the fire drill-elopement story was a non-starter.

An errant alarm, mechanical glitch, nothing more. Waste of a long drive.

But Amy decided to hang around for a while yet, not more than an hour at most, to give a listen. Since she was here already.

She needed to go back to the office with *something*.

But these people seemed dazed, and only Maddie looked to be fully awake.

Amy approached her, "Mind if I ask you some questions?"

Maddie brightened, answering, "We don't usually get the chance, thank you for your interest. Why don't you take me into lunch and we can visit."

Offering her elbow to the reporter, she added: "I could use another arm."

4

Eli

INTENDING TO STRETCH, Eli was on his feet, hovering over the remaining ladies. He wondered what Elora was writing but dared not ask. It looked like a letter. It had been an age since he had cause to write a real letter or receive one that wasn't a bill or a solicitation for "final arrangements."

Instead, he turned to Gladys, who was sitting next to Elora, and sang out: "say, good lookin', whatcha' got cookin'?" Then, bending to her ear with a half-whisper, he confided, "you sure lookin' pretty today. You must be taking those 'pretty pills.'"

Gladys either didn't hear or didn't care to answer.

Elora gave him a side eye. *You believe this?* she thought, not for the first time. *Thinks he's a ladies' man.* They'd both been approached by Eli when he first arrived. Same come-on.

Eli was a small man with a large mustache and an intricate comb-over that he imagined covered his bald spot. He clearly worked on his hair arrangement each morning before stepping out of his room. Apt to come undone at the touch of a breeze or the voicing of even a mild expletive, it never stayed put for long.

"How old do you think I am?" He put the question to the group. "You won't hurt my feelings."

When no one ventured a guess, he answered himself. "I'm eighty-seven."

He was eighty-one. Daniel knew it for a fact.

"Did I ever tell you that I'm from Happy? Happy, Texas?"

Eli kept trying: "I never learned how to dance, I just stand there . . . and lean a little, and love the ladies, and let them move me to the music. Best I can do."

This much was true: he loved to lean on the ladies and dreamt of private instruction. But few had been taken in by his charm, and no one here followed up more than once.

But Eli's mood was far from what most people assumed from his bright chatter.

Mornings, he woke with one question: *Will this be the day?*

Nights, all that week, he had avoided his bed, refusing to stretch out. The only way he could count on a full hour or two of sleep was in his reclining chair, upright, feet elevated, eyes open to the dark. He did not want to be taken by stealth.

Yet night after night, something was taken.

5

Gladys

GLADYS HADN'T BEEN listening when the reporter took Maddie away or when Eli turned his charm upon her earlier (that tired business of "Pretty Pills"). She was staring intently off into some middle distance, distracted by the sudden appearance, disappearance, and reappearance—a flickering image—of two familiar figures approaching. As the flickering subsided, the figures came into focus: her father and mother, posed for a photograph. It was typical of wedding pictures of that time, the man standing stiffly behind the woman, a proprietary hand on her shoulder, his lips severely compressed. Women were usually seated, their faces impossible to read. The image filled her entire field of vision. When tears came to Gladys, as they always did, the image faded. She knew it was not real—not sight but fierce remembrance. The doctor had warned her that it was quite likely a side-effect of a new medication. He urged her to report back on any strange visions or "visitations." He didn't call them "hallucinations," but she knew what he was thinking, and she never reported back to him. These "hallucinations"—whatever you chose to call them—gave her precious company. She wasn't ready to give them up.

6

Elora: I Am Worry

ELORA SETTLED HER handbag. It occupied most of her lap.

When she had to identify it at the library Lost and Found last year, she'd described it as "black, boxy, stylish, shiny like patent leather." She had seen the Queen of England carrying one like it on television. Neat as a pin on the outside—chaos within. Wadded Kleenex and dusty mints, comb, change purse, pillbox, paper packets of sugar and salt (small thefts from the dining room), all swirling together as she poked around for a working pen and a letter in an unstamped envelope she was almost—*finally!*—ready to deliver.

She shut the metal clasp with a smart click and unfolded the much-folded letter; for days she had been fussing over it. The director was her only hope. She needed to remind him politely of his promise to meet with Alexei before it was too late—she would need to be especially careful not to sound pushy in bringing up the subject of her grandnephew again.

> *Thank you for Alexei meeting. I give him your phone number and he told me he will call. I hope he listen to you and go in the right direction. He has no more time in the high school. He is my only close family in America so I am worry. I am here night and day and will be happy to visit with you for five minutes. May I say before you waste your time to listen to his lies please ask him about the book I give him to read. He never touch it. When I told him I bought it for him he said who asked you to buy it. Since you bought it I am not going to read it. He says dont call me Alexei I am Alex.*
>
> *I would like that between you and him you talk to him to bring him back to the right path. From the beginning I did wonders for him but now he does not appreciate. In contrary he is ashamed of me. I did not get married because of him. I thought he won't be taken care of if I was with husband.*
>
> *On this week-end he was at his girl friends to eat and sleep. Pluss he sends her I miss you cards everyday after. I miss your voice, your tender touch, your kiss excetera, excetera. I ask him what work does her father do. He says none of your business. I say her fathers job must not be worthy to mention. Are they a good family why not say? I have seen the pictures he tries to hide from me. They are standing at the lake in bathing suits. She is short her head comes under his arm. . . .*

7

Two by Two: Maddie and Amy

MADDIE STRUGGLED to her feet, offering her elbow to the reporter. Venturing out with only an ordinary cane, she had overestimated her strength once again. Until recently, she had been able to get around on her own two feet, relying on her single cane for backup, and on that extra push needed when shifting from sitting to standing. Lately she was finding that even one of the four-footed canes no longer felt secure.

All of the residents were haunted by the sense of an inevitable downward progression of disability. She saw it all around her, from cane—to rolling walker—to wheelchair—to bedfast—to "perpetual bed." Maddie saw herself in that procession. They were all falling into the earth, one after the other. Their time was coming.

"You're kind of quiet," Amy observed as they shuffled down the path to the residence.

"Wondering what you want to hear," said Maddie after a long pause.

"You know, the olden days," Amy said vaguely.

"Well, you were asking before—'Is this a club?' Far from it. We came together the first time by accident, all of us needing to sit down. That was the only empty bench. Afterwards, we seemed to run into each other at the same time every day, right there. Accidently on purpose, I guess. I don't know why, we don't have anything in common . . . except for being old."

Maddie lurched forward precipitously to point at something on the ground. *A penny, of all things!*

Amy tugged her gently but firmly away from it.

Maddie balked: "It's against my principles to leave money on the ground. 'Find a penny, pick it up—all day long you'll have good luck.'"

"That's superstition!" Amy said, happy to have engaged her. "Guess how much a penny's worth—practically zilch. It's not even copper—it's zinc. It's not worth the trouble of carrying it around."

"Here's where our generations differ. Ever hear of the Great Depression?"

"Some things. . . ."

"You've heard of the Dust Bowl?"

"*That!* Sure."

And now Maddie started to hold forth with energy and conviction. As someone who was raised in the aftermath of the Great Depression and the Dust Bowl, she tried to convey to Amy how hard the hard times could get in America. "We did with what we had. Diced apples for breakfast, water for lunch, swollen bellies for supper" is how she remembered it.

"Ever hear of salt and pepper soup?"

"What's that?"

"What it sounds like. Pinch of pepper, double pinch of salt. Water to taste."

"You're joking, right?"

"Pretty serious joke."

Am I superstitious? Maddie asked herself. True, she kept a few old customs. Back when she had a kitchen, on New Year's Day, for instance, she would always fix a platter of black-eyed peas and cabbage, as her grandmother had. Cabbage for folding money, peas for luck. She did it more for memory's sake than conviction. She had no definite expectations. It's something she did. When she moved into the residence, she had asked the kitchen staff to make it, and they continued the tradition for some years, until that group retired.

8

Elora's Letter

AS BEST AS THEY could piece it together afterwards, this is what happened.

A breeze had struck up. That was part of it. Maddie and the reporter were walking on ahead, Gladys and Eli straggling after them. No one was looking back. Elora and Daniel would follow in a minute, bringing up the rear.

A woman leashed to a small dog passed them. The dog was some sort of terrier mix, a fraction of her size, dragging her from tree to tree. "Wait till I get you to the house, you devil, you!" she cried.

The two of them—the woman who didn't look to be that old but was clearly exhausted, tried beyond her strength, reminded Elora (*again!*) of times with her great-nephew. She thought of Lily, sweet-faced Lily. She'd bought the dog for him (at no small price); Lily was purebred Corgi. She knew that the Queen of England had preferred Corgis. Supposedly she was Alexei's pet, though most of the time she was the only one who fed or walked or talked to the creature. And she couldn't forget how Lily had gone lost before this past Christmas, Alexei telling her that it had happened on purpose—leaving Lily on Santa's lap at the mall. She didn't know whether the part about Santa was true, but this much was: winter had come and gone, and Lily had not returned.

"That thing was a pest," was how Alexei had excused it: "Fat. Ugly. Old."

Right then a boy on a bike came up on Elora's left side and then, in a flash, no longer trailing behind but forging ahead of them, swinging her handbag triumphantly over his head. Daniel was too busy stabilizing Elora and making sure she didn't fall to be able to give chase. Only when he'd escorted Elora back to the bench, and was sure he had her securely seated, was he free to go after the thief.

And there it was!

The patent leather pocketbook! The boy was nowhere in sight, but he'd thrown down the handbag, strewing its contents on the ground, a short distance up the path. Daniel gathered the change purse and compact but judged the lighter paper items, already scattered and blowing, not worth the chase. Besides, he could only leave residents like Elora on her own for a few minutes.

He would decide whether to file a police report later, after he had returned Elora safe and sound to the main residence. He would try to convince her that she had done the sensible thing not to have struggled, risking a dislocated shoulder, or worse, had she tried to yank the thing back.

As it happened, Elora decided for him. No convincing was necessary. They were in agreement that it would be useless to go through all that police paperwork. And what could they say? He never got a look at the thief's face, only his back. And he wasn't really a thief but more a bad kid. And what, come to think of it, had actually been stolen? There was no need for money at Shady Rest, so Elora only kept a few coins in a change purse so that she had an excuse to carry the pocketbook.

Back at the residence, she sought only the privacy of her room. Her refuge: Room 32. She needed to lie down. She wouldn't report the theft—didn't want to think about it for another minute. One glance at her face should have told anyone that much. Solace at the reception desk should have known better than to ask. People were always making arrangements for Elora. Without her. She was wise to their ways.

Safely in bed, Elora drew her handbag close. Her change purse was intact though empty; her compact mirror was cracked, and face powder spilled over everything. Nothing anyone would call "valuable" was missing. Nothing but her precious, painstakingly composed, letter to the director. Must've blown away when the contents spilled—who else would want it?

And now Elora was so very tired. There was nothing left for her to do. Stretched out on the bed, fully dressed, even her shoes—too much of an effort to pull them off, her ankles were so swollen.

As a Medicaid patient, Elora wasn't really entitled to a single room. The arrangement was temporary: this room had become available unexpectedly, and since Elora was known to be "difficult," she'd been placed here until they could find a suitable roommate for her elsewhere. It would not be easy.

The room appeared unlived-in. It was one of the larger ones and seemed larger still, since she had left what furniture she intended to pass on in Alexei's keeping.

Only the framed photographs on top of the dresser gave the room the least personal touch. One was of Alexei as a child when he was still sweet to her. When would that have been? Nine at most.

They're at a beach. The sea at their backs is calm and bright. Alexei is wrapped in a towel. Elora and he lean together, his head comes under her arm. The other photo is Alexei a year or two older, standing alone, squinting, staring—as she'd always warned him not to—directly at the sun.

She took out her teeth, her upper dentures, and dropped them into the water glass on her bedside table, then pulled the hospital blanket up to her chin. She closed her eyes, hoping that anyone checking in on her would think she was asleep, or at least resting peacefully, and decide not to disturb her.

Her pose was not convincing to the head nurse or any of the aides who looked in on her later. With only her lower teeth in place, her jaw jutted out; she looked fiercely-aggrieved, granite in resolve—anything but peaceful.

Her decision was made. She would not budge. No, she would not write that letter again.

9

Dining Room: Ask Me

ON HIS WAY back from settling Elora in her room, Daniel noticed a small crowd forming around the dining room entrance. A woman with scorched red hair, whose name escaped him, was blocking the *Menu for the Week* posted on the door, reading it out loud, including the days already past, meals already consumed.

"What's up?" Daniel stepped in to clear the passageway: "Is there a problem? Shouldn't be—it's pulled pork today—a big favorite."

"I can't eat pork," she explained. "The Bible says so—it's in the Bible—God wrote the Bible. Who knows better than God?"

The logic was air-tight. Daniel had learned to avoid arguments like this. The kitchen staff was well aware to have plenty of back-ups ready—someone always had a complaint or objection. Daniel promised to go back and remind them anyway.

Amy and Maddie were staked out at a quiet corner table where they hoped to resume their conversation. *Simply a conversation so far—practice for the real thing. Not yet an interview,* Amy reminded herself.

Nothing would be served for at least thirty minutes, but, as was customary, the dining room was starting to fill up well in advance. One of the kitchen workers was making more noise than necessary putting down plates and utensils. The clang and clatter were as clear as outright speech, telling them how much she resented having to work around people who had nothing better to do than sit and gawk and get in the way. *Other people have to work!* The woman, noticeably stooped and moving with pained stiffness, seemed to be none too young herself.

"Mind my recording a little?" Amy positioned her recorder closer to Maddie, who was speaking much too softly. "This little gadget is my traveling secretary and my best friend. I depend on her, that's why I have to test that she's working properly. Is that okay?"

"I know what a tape recorder is," Maddie countered. But now she was so self-conscious at the prospect of being recorded that it was hard to get started.

"How do people fill their time, living here?"

"Oh, child."

How to explain? We breathe. We dream. We remember. We talk to people, and sometimes they answer. We laugh. We weep. Like you, we don't stop.

"You know how that fairy tale ending goes?" Maddie asks.

Dining Room: Ask Me

"You mean about living happily ever after?"

"No. Another one—it's less well known: 'And if they have not died, they are living still.' We're still alive, you know."

Ask me! Maddie thinks that if the reporter really wanted to know, she'd be asking tougher questions. Like the questions Maddie keeps asking herself: did you find what you were looking for? Do you still long for anything? If the longing has faded, what replaces it? (Are you angry? Do you feel cheated? Did you deserve more?)

When, on the morning of her husband's last birthday, she presented him with these very questions, Al fell silent and stared at his lap. Maddie had prepared his favorite breakfast—blueberry pancakes, real maple syrup, fresh-brewed coffee with real cream. She'd arranged these delicacies formally with a cloth napkin on a tray. He pushed the tray away.

When she asked him: "What is it you want, Al? I can't tell anymore," he answered quietly: "Everything."

Refusing to touch anything on the tray, he studied his fingernails instead—she noticed they bulged strangely. Then Maddie knew he would not live to see out the year.

Wishing and wanting to go on and on. Maddie imagined trying to communicate this to Amy now. How wanting so strongly for things doesn't count. This girl will have to learn in her own life, in her own good time. No one can learn it for her.

Maddie had been a teacher; she loved explaining things. *I probably overdid it sometimes.*

"If wishes were horses, beggars would ride." Maddie couldn't help herself. Amy stared back, puzzled, a frown line formed and as quickly faded, her face so smooth and untroubled—so young! It occurred to Maddie that her own granddaughter (if her daughter Rachel had lived to have children) would have been much the same age as Amy now. There might have been the same gulf of misunderstanding between them.

The assignment had been a bust, but Amy needed to salvage something from the morning. There had to be a story around here somewhere: the question was whether anyone was willing to tell it and, if so, would anyone want to read it? Was there a feel-good angle here? Looking around the dining room, she didn't think so.

How about … a profile of a few of the residents, the ones known to be reliable. A series of mini-memoirs? The idea wasn't so far-fetched. They all have memories, right? Except for those in the special section down the hall for those who don't. . . .

She would think it over on her long drive back to the office. But the number of permissions she would need: the director, the residents, that guy Dan—or was it Stan?

Dining Room: Ask Me

Amy was not convinced that it was worthwhile spending one more minute on a conversation that might never pan out.

Right then, as if on cue, Amy's phone rang. She excused herself to take the call in the hallway where it would be quieter.

The gist of the matter turned out to be this: the city editor had lost a reporter and needed someone to drive out to the fairground and cover the annual chili cook-off, plus a bunch of other competitive eating events. Last year's all-round grand champion eater (speed and volume) had thrown his fork into the ring again. Speaking figuratively, of course. In point of fact, he was famous for using his hands, never a fork or any kind of utensil; he simply tore the meat with his teeth and used all ten fingers to shovel the rest in.

"Plenty of free samples," the editor concluded. "Should be fun."

It was a no-brainer.

Maddie noticed that the girl was smiling when she returned from the hall. There was a curious nibbling quality to her laugh that suggested she was holding something back. It was pretty obvious how relieved she was to be called away.

"Sorry . . . breaking news," would have to be sufficient excuse.

"It never stops." Amy sighed. "Got to go now. But I'll be back."

"*You* might be," Maddie said, tearing off a strip of leftover bread and rolling it into pill shapes.

"It's a rain check, I promise," Amy said without conviction.

"At my age, I don't make promises." She had wanted to resume their conversation and had hoped to convince Amy that this last age was not an impoverishment—on the contrary, there were good things to be said about it. If only by virtue of coming last and encompassing all the ages and stages that had come before, it was bound to be the richest for reflection, at least for those who cared to reflect.

But then again, for the young, how could any of that compare with life pounding upon their pulses—right now, this minute.

Amy extended her hand to Maddie in parting, and when Maddie took it, she couldn't miss Amy's faint recoil. Did this young woman think old age was contagious? But Maddie bit her tongue, reminding herself that she was not a bitter person.

By now the dining room was mostly filled. Amy caught a flash of fire—the red-headed woman was sitting alone at a table for two, spoon already in hand, watching the servers lay out the lunch dessert buffet, eyeing the selection with suspicion.

On her way out, Amy was struck by how many of the tables, even the larger ones, were occupied by

Dining Room: Ask Me

people looking down at their plates, eating silently as though by themselves.

Maddie also chose to dine solo, remaining at the table for four in the quiet corner that Amy had picked out for their interview. She wasn't hungry, but she went through the motions, saying to herself: *You have to keep up your strength, regular habits steady us,* and such.

But right now, it wouldn't have felt true. She's not up to persuading anyone of anything. Instead, she remained, pushing the table settings aside. She continued rolling the remaining scraps of bread into pellets, then mashing them into shapelessness.

Her mood was darkening. *All paid up and nowhere to go* was the feeling.

10

Admission

HIS NAME WAS Wiktor, not Victor. His last name, starting with the letters "Cz," was too difficult. "Wiktor" it would have to be.

Daniel was perfectly familiar with the intake protocol and shouldn't have been nervous, but he was. A nurse recorded Wiktor's vital signs on a clipboard and handed it off to Daniel. He knew it was highly unusual to bring a patient into the Board Room. Few if any of the junior staff ever entered it. But this day, with meetings everywhere else . . . it was available, it would have to do.

The new resident was eighty-three years old, recently widowed, and childless. Only natural to assume (hope) that these circumstances would make him a suitable fit with the other "orphans"—Eli, Elora, Gladys, and Maddie—also without family.

A person of some distinction, apparently, in a field of specialization which wouldn't mean much here.

Admission

He'd been an indexer for a number of academic publishers in the days before computers took over, when many indexes were still crafted by hand, ending up as an archivist in the rare book collection of a university library. He'd lived in Chicago for all of his working life. He and his wife Helen had retired here in Brewster because his wife, who was from a local family, cherished happy memories of growing up in the area. At the time, her remaining relatives seemed to be in good health. Then one by one they passed on and eventually his wife as well. Wiktor had no other connection with this town, no history here; it never became more than a place on the map. In her last years (with connections dwindling), even Helen felt herself a stranger here.

"Listen more, speak less," Daniel's grandma had liked to say: "Why do you think you were given two ears and only one mouth?" He had been listening, intently, but Wiktor wasn't saying much.

There were times when Wiktor felt as divided and dispersed as the Dodo, that ill-fated—what was it, bird? fowl? landfish?—now extinct, with a foot in the British Museum in London and a head in Copenhagen. This had been one of those times.

Just then, Wiktor felt the approach of a dyskinesia episode (one of his body's many betrayals) and moved around somewhat manically in an effort to conceal it. He had hoped to avoid the issue of Parkinson's Disease until it was necessary and here it was, revealing itself the very first day, in his admission interview.

Unsteadily, he made his way to the glass-fronted cabinets that lined the walls of the room, its shelves full of medical tomes written by members of the Board of Trustees. He halted for mere seconds before a display of rare vintage editions of *Casket and Sunnyside*, the journal of mortuary management. It might have been expected that he would take an archival interest in these rare volumes, but instead he headed over to a cabinet filled with anatomical specimens in what appeared to be pickling jars. He leaned in close and lingered. What had so captured his interest? Nothing much—as far as Daniel, peering over Wiktor's shoulder, was able to observe. A bloated, bleached-out appendix. Several brains (*former residents?* Wiktor wondered), each in its own bottle. *Why stall here?* Wiktor did not say, and Daniel did not ask. Instead, he followed Wiktor in silence, holding his clipboard to his chest like a shield.

Last week, Wiktor had been reading about the latest developments in both hibernation therapy and cryogenics. Hibernation he dismissed as bunk. But Americans, apparently, were embracing cryogenics and having themselves beheaded as a way of outwitting death. Freezing the head was a bargain, because whole body preservation was prohibitively expensive. Only think of the warehousing—storage into the indefinite future while they worked out the kinks. Neither procedure was the least bit painful—according to the article. The patient was disconnected a few minutes before actual death and submerged in a vat of liquid nitrogen at sub-zero temperatures.

Wiktor moved on to admire a kidney which had not lost its color.

"It started with a fall," Wiktor answered after a long pause. Then checked himself. "Well, that's not exactly how it happened." First came the "senior moments," familiar words seeping away, sometimes irrecoverably. "The damage" started with a fall. To be precise: perhaps the damage was the hip fracture *unmasked* by the fall. Life itself was the damage.

"Are you in discomfort now?" Daniel asked.

When Wiktor frowned and did not answer, Daniel realized the problem was with his choice of the word: *discomfort*.

"Better if I call it 'pain'? Can you rate the pain you are feeling on a scale of one to ten?"

Daniel, a quick learner, knew enough to refrain from giving Wiktor the emoji pain chart with the faces.

"You want me to tell you how many units precisely?" Wiktor's tone was condescending, distinctly mocking: "One: almost negligible; ten: sheer misery?"

The problem was more with not *feeling*, Wiktor reflected. This null space, this unaliveness. After the broken bones healed, numbness set in. Anti-depressants and anti-anxiety medications were prescribed. The numbness—if that's what it was—was worse than the pain. Afraid of actually forgetting it, he practiced saying his wife's name out loud on waking and throughout the empty spaces of the day.

Helen. Her name was Helen.

One of the specialists he'd been referred to was of the opinion that people lose the ability to mourn by the time they reached their eighties. From sheer overload: too many funerals and losses at this point in their lives. The doctor added that he was not familiar with any scientific study confirming his theory. There were no hard numbers, but it was plausible enough.

Along with the sorrow Wiktor did or did not feel, there was an enormous disappointment. His colleagues—all learned men—had proved to be weak and inconstant, as dazed and unprepared for the devastation already in their midst—as much as ordinary men. They were nearly all gone now. Swept away as the sages warned, as a flood sweeps away a sleeping village, their lifetime labors—small grains, scattered.

Prognosis: Months / Weeks / Days / Hours. Daniel stared blankly at the form, for he was starting to drift. Now, of all times, he found himself recalling this morning's dream. He needed to find his glasses, it started with this. He'd run back to the house, but all he could find were half-lenses, fragments of glass. He wanted to drive his grandparents home while he could still see the way, before it got completely dark, and he needed his own glasses! Strange, Daniel thought, because he had never worn glasses.

But he hadn't been listening and now was caught stealing a glance at his wrist, a hint of timekeeping. Wiktor, noticing this and clearly miffed, was ready to leave.

Admission

Naptime. The hallway was deserted. Most of the residents had retreated to their rooms. With Wiktor pausing to read, or pretending to read, the wall plaques for "Perpetual Beds," his progress was painfully slow. What could his interest be in Suzi Schiffer, Clayton Townsend, Victoria Godfrey, Salvador "Apache" Serrano, the names of total strangers?

Anyone he knows?

Apparently not, so he moved on—to honors and framed tributes to volunteers. He moved so slowly the corridor seemed very long indeed. Still more "Perpetual Beds." They passed a closet-sized library of donated books.

"Is this a library?" More observation than question.

Daniel surprised himself by answering defensively: "It's a fact that reading takes a lot of concentration." He left it at that.

They passed the common room where television news was being broadcast to vacant chairs. Standing in the open door, facing out, a distraught woman in a shower cap:

"Turn off the war and let me go home! Tell his Hanoi Honey that I don't care!"

Daniel steered Wiktor away.

Turning left into the residence proper, Daniel paused at Wiktor's door, to give him a moment to appreciate the hard work of the staff. As a welcome, new residents were always greeted with a decorated door to their room. In this case, they had researched and found a photo of Wiktor in younger, healthier days and had even written out his name in an old-English script, despite the fact that his native language was Polish.

Like boarding school, maybe a college dorm.

Thoughtful. But was it, really? Wiktor imagined the custom was designed to help lost and confused residents find their rooms when wandering the halls. But that assumed that the residents would recognize their faces from fifty years ago. Wiktor didn't think he had ever met the man in the picture on his door.

Daniel pointed out the special features of this room: the light dimmers, the temperature controls, call buttons, at both bedside and commode, then, feeling it had been enough—more than enough for one day—prepared to take his leave. He heard Wiktor's thoughts as clearly as if he had spoken out loud: *Let it rest*.

"Want the door open or closed?" A formality. Daniel knew the answer without having to ask.

"Closed, please!" Wiktor replied, making no effort to disguise his relief at the prospect of a little privacy.

Settling in, alone at last, Wiktor found a copy of the in-house bulletin open and waiting on his pillow. The mission statement on the cover affirmed that it was written and published by the residents, calling themselves "guests."

"We, the guests at Shady Rest, are made to feel that we are not forgotten and still in the stream of life, with entertainment, arts and crafts, exercise, and trips, fun and special friendships...."

Admission

"Our deepest regrets are extended to the families of—"

"... winner of this week's Crossword Challenge, John Eisendrath!"

More names that meant nothing to him.

"Those who attended the latest trip to the art museum. ..."

Also, *"our condolences to—"*

"... the proud members of the Gourmet Cooking Club. Next week, Lisa Tucek will battle Kimmie Walker in the annual Jello-Bowl! Most original Jello salad wins! (Remember Lisa, folks? She packs a mean marshmallow!")

It has come to this.

A final paragraph devoted to the *"senior-most resident, Freda Green ... 99 years and counting. Her secrets for long life—forthcoming in a later issue."*

II

11

A Day in Spring

THEY COULDN'T HAVE asked for a prettier day: the trees frothing with new leaves, new grass crowding out the old, every least thing spangled with sunlight.

"Deep breath, everybody!" Daniel couldn't help himself; he wanted everyone to appreciate the moment.

It was warm for April. School was done for the day, and the small park was swarming. Kids raced by on scooters and skateboards, a menace to slower pedestrians, but the members of Daniel's group were out of the way, safely parked on the sidelines, seated on their bench. Their faces moved with the sun like sunflowers, yet even when shining in full sunlight, they remained invisible to those passing. A dozen tots from a nearby nursery school went by, chirping to themselves. The children marched two abreast while holding fast to a rope that lassoed them in at waist level. Two adults, one holding fore, one aft, steered their progress, orderly so far. They moved as a unit.

Overhead, underfoot, birds were buzzing and chattering. The same birds as last season or new ones? Did it matter? A blackbird poked around Maddie's feet as though among stones. Sparrows crowded a patch of pavement near the bench where someone must have dropped crumbs. Sparrows or wrens, Daniel guessed, but he'd never bothered to learn their particular names—all small brown birds were "sparrows" to him, all blackbirds were "crows."

"Seems like they're saying *'tseek . . . seek!"* Maddie observed.

"Sounds more like *'took . . . took!'* to me," said Daniel. "Do you suppose they're arguing?"

Right then, a big beautiful blue bird—harsh-voiced and bullying—swooped down on them, crying (as far as Eli could tell): "*Drop it!*" and "*Pull it up!*"

"They speak—but not to us," Wiktor said wistfully.

Yet people are so much more interesting, Maddie thought. A young woman approached wearing a dark blue T-shirt with the word *BLESSED* emblazoned in bold white letters across her well-endowed chest. *What's her story?* Maddie smiled and waved to her. The woman waved briefly back but without slowing down and was soon past them.

Gladys also preferred watching people to birds. *They're all beautiful, especially the children. They don't know it, but they are.*

When Maddie said something about it being a pity for anyone to miss such a fine day, the others suspected she was thinking of one person in particular. For

Elora was no longer with them, and by now everyone knew her story.

How a young man, her only surviving family member, had arrived at her bedside on her last day and was overheard weeping and shouting, "I know you're inside there!" when Elora refused, or was no longer able, to open her eyes. It had become another one of those cautionary tales: how she'd lost hope after her handbag was stolen and taken to her bed, refusing food and drink from that day on. "Died of discouragement, short and simple," was the verdict—despite the fact that she'd gotten her bag back almost immediately and nothing of value had been taken.

When Daniel had visited her, Elora did not acknowledge his presence either. Her hands were balled up, her fingers bunched, closed in on themselves. Days before, a physical therapist had tried to pry her fingers loose and insert a rubber ball but gotten nowhere with it. Elora was holding fast to all she had left—which was exactly nothing.

"It's hell getting old," said Eli.

"Considering the alternative. . . ." Wiktor completed his thought. He tended to speak formally, in a lecturing tone, even when uttering commonplaces. Eli took it personally; he felt condescended to and replied with what small sarcasm he could muster:

"That's some choice! Like asking: Would you rather go blind or deaf?"

"I've noticed that people who are very sociable fear deafness more; it's more isolating," Maddie joined in.

"Then again," she added, "losing your memory might be the most terrible thing."

"Unless and until you forget you've forgotten," Wiktor amended. "Which happens. A blessing and curse wrapped in one. 'I have forgotten all my hardship and all my father's house.'" And to remind them that he was quoting Scripture, he named chapter and verse.

Eli seemed more than usually restless that morning. He sat for a few minutes, then stood, then paced before sitting down again. He jingled his pocket change, then dug out a key, fingered it lovingly, a key to a home no longer his, a house he had not entered in years, an address he had recently forgotten.

Gladys brought along her knitting bag. Placing it on her lap, she extracted the cross-stitch she had been working on, a blue cloth stretched on a hoop frame with red, yellow, and green threads dangling. A garden scene was partly filled in with tulips and pansies. It was intended to decorate a throw pillow for her favorite niece, but now that Ellen had passed, she couldn't think of whom else to give it to. She feared idleness, though, and dark thoughts. Cross-stitch kept her occupied. And it was soothing, simply the doing of it. The repeated over-and-under stabbing motion calmed her. So she persisted. Truthfully, she couldn't stop. Always the same pattern, they piled up under her bed: hidden gifts, ungiven.

A Day in Spring

What Gladys feared most was stroke—it ran in the family, both sides. Her father died with one word on his lips. For years, it was only that one word, and it was a curse: all he had left to serve for all occasions. One cousin suffered a kinder fate, but not to be wished for, even so. His only word was "Oh!"—neither happy nor unhappy—uttered each time with astonishment.

But even when speech remained, words failed to bridge the distance at the end.

When her mother's time came, she had spoken clearly. Two words: "Hold on!"

Gladys and her sister, standing at their mother's bedside, were deeply puzzled by this. Her mother's head was turned away from them and to the wall. The wall was perfectly blank. Gladys took her mother's hand and held on—until she understood that what seemed a solid wall must have been an opening to the Other Side, the far shore, where her father and brother had come out to meet her, and that her mother was speaking to *them* on the other side, telling *them* to "hold on . . . wait a little"—she'd be coming to them as soon as she could get free. It was exactly the opposite of what Gladys had thought the words meant.

Then and only then did Gladys let go of her mother's hand.

"Tell us something cheerful," Daniel suggested. "A surprise visit . . . a good dream"—but he was answered with silent, staring faces. He couldn't always predict what subjects would tick them off. When Daniel feared losing the group to private reverie, he sometimes got desperate and was liable to clutch at any subject that offered itself at that moment, anything to keep the conversation going.

But there were some obvious subjects to avoid. And sometimes he wasn't the one to blame; he wasn't the one to get them started.

It was Wiktor who set them off last weekend—a feature article in the Saturday supplement detailing the last meal of the latest executed prisoner in the state. A murderer with a giant's appetite, he had ordered doubles on every item on the menu (chicken-fried steak, English peas, home fries), triples on desert (three kinds of cobbler topped with whipped cream), all to be washed down with a pitcher of Cherry Coke. The prison officials followed his instructions to the letter but, when the feast was spread before him, he pushed it away. Refused to take a bite.

"What happened to all that good food?" Gladys got quite worked up about it. Daniel had never seen her so energized. "Did it go to waste? All that good food and all their work getting it ready! Did he refuse to touch it from spite? And then what happened? Did the guards divide up the meal and eat it themselves? Or did nobody want to touch it?"

No one knew.

For Eli's sake they would be leaving a few minutes early. He had hinted, then started walking off on his own, announcing: "Got to go to the little room." So they all got going.

Daniel couldn't help noticing what, only a few days ago, Eli had coyly referred to as the "little boys' room" had suffered an erasure to become the "little room," although the room was far from small. There had been other troubling lapses of late—like calling the television set the "bandbox" and struggling with familiar place settings, coming out with "knobs" for knife and fork. In time—should this process continue—not even Daniel would be able to translate what he meant to say. It would be up to the Memory Care Unit to figure it out.

12

Lunch in Memory Care

DANIEL DECIDED TO take his lunch in the Memory Care Unit. Three of the nurses there had been especially friendly and welcoming to him. They were called "The Weather Sisters" because the nicknames they went by were "Sunny," "Misty," and "Rainy." Sunny had the darkest skin and the brightest disposition. She wasn't strictly "Black" or "African-American." That was according to the online ancestry research outfit she consulted, one of those deals where you pay to spit in a cup, mail it into a DNA lab, and get to learn who your great-great grandparents were. Turned out, there was more Mexican in her mix—and Quanah Parker fit in there someplace.

"Misty" was a pallid ash blonde when she remembered to cover the grey. The third "sister" was light-skinned, called "Rainy" because her real name was Renee. Far from being sisters, the three were not even remotely related—their meeting up here in middle age was due to sheer chance.

Today they were curious to learn more about Wiktor, the latest admission to the residence. With his distinguished looks—perfect posture and full head of silver hair—he was as handsome as a man his age could hope to be. His unpronounceable last name helped pique their interest and his aloofness heightened the mystery. "He's a cold fish," had been the consensus among the few residents who had tried to introduce themselves. Sunny wondered if it wasn't simply shyness.

"I think it's Parkinson's," Daniel suggested.

Wiktor reminded Misty of a patient she had taken care of years ago when she worked for a private agency. He was also a foreigner and standoffish and had some strange habits like insisting that tomatoes and grapes must be peeled before eating. "It's *savage* not to," he told her.

Rainy, who usually lacked an experience to offer up, knew a thing or two about Parkinson's that she was eager to share: a few years ago, she had been assigned a patient that had such extreme Parkinsonian dyskinesia, that she knocked her own teeth out with her own knees.

"Really!" Rainy insisted. Evidently, dentures replaced the missing teeth, but after a third such event, she had been relieved of her remaining teeth and was prescribed a no-chew diet.

"I swear," Rainy insisted again, discouraged by their silence.

Sunny filled the void: "In this line of work you're sure to meet all kinds."

But what else does Daniel know about Wiktor?

"Not much. I know that he's alone."

"Aren't the others?" Misty asked.

"More than most," Daniel said. "All alone."

"What'd he do in life?" Misty asked.

"Isn't he in *life* now?" he asked back.

"You know what Misty means—why so grumpy today?" Sunny put in.

Daniel admitted that he was tired. "It's been a long day and it's barely half over."

To those who had never been to the Memory Care Unit, it might have come as a surprise to learn that it wasn't an entirely cheerless place. True, it was a locked ward. Also true, the staff kept their lunches locked up. Candies were kept in maximum security in the nurse's locked desk drawers, after an unfortunate incident with a diabetic patient. Sweets were as guarded as the contents of the computerized medication cart.

The nurses' station was the hub, panoptic, and the patients' rooms rayed off from the main desk like the spokes of a wheel. Yet the mood overall was far from gloomy. Forgetting can also be an unburdening. Daniel remembered the scripture that Wiktor had recited: "I have forgotten all my hardship and all my father's house...."

Daniel unwrapped his sandwich. Swiss cheese on whole wheat, no lettuce, bread slathered with mayo, two cookies, and an apple for dessert. A creature of habit, he ate the same thing every working day (for efficiency's sake), wrapping it up and stowing it in the fridge the last thing before going to bed. No variation. He didn't want to have to decide or choose or think about other possibilities.

The subject of Freda Green came up as it usually did: whether she would make it to the actual day of her birthday and, if she didn't last until then, whether the staff could handle the disappointment after whipping up all the expectation. And what about her "children" who must be in their seventies and not doing so well themselves? It was a wait and see—they didn't want to get anyone's hopes up only to have them dashed. And what no one wanted to ask out loud: was it worth it, the pain and the trouble of living so long? And, *really*—isn't this the stinger—outliving so many others?

There was constant interruption in this ward. Discipline was lax because it was impossible. A man in a wheelchair introduced himself to Daniel as "John." Asked about his last name, he didn't seem much troubled by drawing a blank: "If I'd've remembered it, I would've said it. Maybe tomorrow it'll come back to me." John waved his hand expansively over their table, now strewn with sandwich wrappings and crumpled napkins. He announced: "This is my treat, don't forget. I'm picking up the check."

In many respects, The Weather Sisters had an easier time of it than Daniel with his own "high-functioning" charges, who noticed so much more and complained and kept a strict tally of grudges and gripes.

Their attempts at conversation were continually interrupted. The overhead television, always on, didn't help. And Daniel had a bad habit of tuning out from time to time. Sunny noticed it especially today.

"Penny for your thoughts," she said.

"I never did understand what that's supposed to mean," Daniel confessed. "I've heard it before."

"It means your thoughts are worth something."

"Can't be much," Daniel objected. "Considering what a penny's worth...."

Patients (it's all right to call them "patients" in *this* unit) kept milling around them as the staffers finished eating and clearing the table, the drumbeat of breaking news breaking over their heads all the while, its rhythm a heartbeat, regular and relentless, to which few attended. It colored their mood, nonetheless.

The day's top story was about climate change, global warming, proceeding at an accelerating pace—a million species, if the experts were to be believed, racing to extinction. Sea stars roamed the ocean unmoored, lost, their tidal pools evaporating....

On his walk back to the Residence, Daniel noticed a young girl reading a children's book to one of the patients. It must be her grandmother or great-grandmother. They looked familiar to him, but no names came to mind.

The story they were reading, *Goodnight Moon*, was meant for the very young. Daniel's grandmother had read it to him every night for years, long past the age considered appropriate. Night after night, he had insisted on it. It became a stay against the dark, against the vanishing of everything he knew and loved. Maybe it was the constancy of the litany, the ritual, that soothed and reassured him, a fearful child fighting sleep. He would let go of each object in the room only after saying goodnight to it. Goodnight to kittens and mittens, the moon in the window, a little old lady bedside, whispering "Hush. . . ."

"And here comes your most favorite part," the girl prompted. "It's one of the rhyming ones: remember kittens and mittens?" The old woman frowned. "Goodnight comb, and goodnight brush. . . . A bowl of what? It rhymes with brush—"

The ancient face lit up. "Mush!" she sang out, beaming.

They both clapped.

13

You Are Here

BACK IN THE main building, Daniel spotted Eli at the other end of the corridor; even at a distance, he recognized the corkscrew gait. It looked like he was toiling uphill—and, come to think of it, he had gotten in the habit lately of saying he was going "up" to the dining room or "down" to Bingo when everything was laid out on one level. It was all perfectly flat.

Why now did he come to a sudden stop halfway down the hall?

No mystery: midway between the Memory Care Unit and the Residence was a large, framed map. As he stood there, Eli seemed to be negotiating something. He jabbed at the glass with his finger; his lips moved.

The map said YOU ARE HERE. *How did they know?*

"You" means "I." "Here" means "There"—red arrow, other side of the glass.

It made no sense!

His gaze kept drifting off the map. Outwards, over the edge of the frame. *Here be dragons....* He flattened the ball of his thumb against the red arrow to anchor it. But no dragons—unless maybe—this little one, this grey, dusty Miller moth trapped in the bottom corner behind the glass.

But where's Happy? It should be here! My Happy Happy home? What sort of map is this?

"*You are here*"—but where is "*here*"? Any which way you turn, it's the same deal. Nowhere else to go. White coats asking the same pesky question over and over: "Can you spell 'world' backwards? W-O-R-L-D?"

"Why would I want to? "

"Can't or won't?" The white coats pressed.

Now, here in the hallway, something else strange was happening. Was one leg shrinking? Eli caught himself listing to one side. He had been off balance for some time. For how long? Days? Weeks? *Should have written down the date he first noticed it.*

And how did he get "Here" in the first place?

He'd set out with clear purpose. Something to do with Wiktor—hoping to run into him. He needed to continue their unfinished conversation but could not recall what they'd been talking about.

The common room looked empty. Eli ducked inside. To "collect his wits." Did people still say this?

Daniel still had a few precious minutes left over from his lunch break. He walked down the hall with purpose, worried that the double doors to the common room might be open and someone in there, bored or lonely or both, would hail him and try to engage him. And so it was—it was Eli who noticed him and waved.

"Only got a minute," he cautioned as Eli patted the chair next to him by way of invitation. But his resolve quickly deflated. He was fond of Eli.

The room was dark, the chairs lined up as though it was movie night. Eli was alone, seated smack in the middle of the empty rows.

But, strangely, the television was not on. Nothing going on.

Daniel was unnerved. After a brief search he found the remote under Eli's seat and turned the TV on. They continued staring at the television in silence at first, until Eli started to laugh. He wagged a finger at the screen where a young woman was extolling the virtues of *Morning Joy*—must be a laxative, but they're too polite to say—as she leapt from her chair and danced away from the breakfast table, skirt swirling.

"That awful woman!" Eli cried. "A new leaf on lice—ha!"

"Lice?" Daniel echoed.

"Life—lease on life! What d'you think I said?"

But Daniel knew what he had heard.

Then it was the same news loop that was on in the Memory Unit: global warming, shrinking habitats, extinction of species. Sea stars roam the oceans adrift, dreaming of tidal pools, safety, containment. *Did someone mention that birds are also leaving?*

And now there was a new Chinese flu. Daniel, too, was drifting.

Where will I be a year from now? he wondered.

Where will anyone here be? he thought more expansively.

A local ad came on:

> *Have you lived a good life?*
> *Then you don't want granite,*
> *You want bronze....*

He started this job after his grandparents passed, both under his care. Their deaths were peaceful and at home. That would be a year ago, come August. Working here was a way of marking time until he was able to decide what he wanted to do with his life. It fitted his needs for now. The woman who interviewed Daniel for the job had taken to him right away because, she explained, male orderlies and aides were so hard to come by and male patients tended to be more comfortable with them.

"Oftentimes men make the best caregivers; they have the strongest backs and biggest hearts."

Then, too, his background—what she called his "attitude" and "upbringing"—were so unusual. "For a young man like you choosing to be your grandparents' caregiver during their last years, that's rare"—all in the best ways, for the best reasons.

Daniel had never considered that he had "chosen" to be their caregiver. He didn't think like that. And he wasn't sure he would have chosen it if he had realized he had a choice.

Young people—the kids he'd gone to school with—had given up urging Daniel to "get a life!" They'd moved on—to jobs, some to college, some even starting families.

How could they be expected to understand what he, himself, struggled to understand?

When now and then someone asked if his job was "boring," Daniel would answer: "Most of the time, you bet! I appreciate 'boring.'" But the question always gave him pause. Weren't they really asking: "Is this enough for you?" And in that pause, he might reply: "Why wouldn't it be?"

From the time of the car crash that killed his parents when he was only an infant, Daniel had lived with his grandparents; they were the only family he'd ever known. He was used to old people, understood their ways—slow and safe. As far back as he could remember, he'd been protected—"over-protected," some said. And for another reason: as a child, his grandmother had impressed upon him, and anyone else who would listen, that he had a "bad" heart (medically speaking), a murmur and arrythmia. He had been excused from Phys Ed at school and prohibited from running at recess. He became the kind of boy who wore stiff leather lace up shoes, while everyone else wore sneakers.

How was he to know if these restrictions were necessary? He was a child, after all. But also, what child would have been so compliant? Truthfully, it had made him feel special and cared for. And by now, caution had become part of his nature. He still wouldn't run in real life. But he ran in his dreams. All the time.

A sense of endless debt was part of it. He recalled a newspaper clipping his grandparents had stowed away with their other keepsakes. Must be in one of those boxes—he must find it.

Packing up to move was the first time he'd seen the clipping. He hadn't imagined it; he'd actually held it in his hands and then lost it somehow. The paper was yellowed and brittle. There was no story attached, only a photograph and caption above the cutline: *Local Infant Saved In Fatal Crash*. The baby was wrapped in what looked like a black blanket with tassels—blood, most likely. If not about himself, why had this clipping been preserved and the story cut away from it? Covered with blood not his own, cushioned by others, he'd been saved. He owed and owed and owed.

Was this what Sunny meant when she had called him an "old soul"? He didn't know what that was, exactly. Something to do with astrology? With reincarnation? Daniel didn't believe in either, but he trusted that Sunny meant it seriously and respectfully—it was not a tease.

14

Long Day

BRIANNA HOUSE was the name of the woman in the wheelchair, the latest candidate for admission to Shady Rest. Daniel had nearly completed the paperwork, but Brianna was struggling with the last item on the questionnaire—a small empty space under the heading *Childhood*.

"They haven't left much room for it," her daughter observed.

"Don't need none," Brianna said, "never had a childhood."

"Now, Mo-ther," the daughter soothed. "Let's not . . . ."

"We'll get back to this later," Daniel suggested, reaching to take the form back. It had been a long day, and he had yet to take a break.

Brianna, along with her daughter and son-in-law, were completing a tour of the living areas and grounds with Daniel as their guide. It had been slow going—coercion thinly disguised as persuasion, the way Daniel saw it.

He was no salesman. The sense of putting on a performance tired him out. Once again, he had resorted to mentioning Freda Green's upcoming hundredth birthday, using it as a selling point—as though such an event were nothing out of the usual around here. Everything he said after this sounded inflated or false to his own ears, too hearty by half.

A few things needed no hype: the back patio with everything blooming in season, for instance, and the sundial with its inscription, "We count none but sunny days."

That day the dining room had been unusually lively. Residents were bartering three choice desserts: brownie for cobbler, ice cream for brownie—calling forth smiles all around.

But the whirlpool bath evinced genuine fear. No argument from Daniel or her own family could convince Brianna that she'd never be left alone to drown in it.

In the dayroom, Brianna gravitated to the upright piano. She doubled over, stretching to reach the keys. The instrument needed tuning, the sound was rumbling, blurred, but it was safe to assume that her hearing was no longer what it had been.

"Can't play without pedals!" she complained.

Daniel stooped to free her feet from the footrests and to wheel her in closer to the keyboard so she could reach the pedals.

And she did—breaking into a spirited, resounding rendition of "In the Garden."

Her daughter and son-in-law joined in on the chorus:

> And He walks with me, and He talks with me,
> and He tells me I am His own,
> and the joy we share, as we tarry there,
> none other has ever known.

And, mysteriously, everything changed after this. It was that exact moment in the day that the light hit the stained glass panels and created a rainbow that filled the room. It seemed providential. "For God's unbroken promise, I knew it!"—Brianna wiped her eyes. There was her theme. Daniel breathed a sigh of relief: she was sold, he could feel it. Until Brianna turned to him:

"Do you know Him?"

"'Course he does!" Sunny, standing in the doorway, seemed to have materialized out of thin air. The nick of time—a narrow escape. Sunny would take over from here. She was known to be the clincher.

No such luck with Daniel's next assignment, but it would be his last for the day. Robert Heppler had a well-earned reputation for mulishness, in a place where the competition was stiff—and for brutal frankness, where he stood unrivaled. To the perfectly polite routine question "How are you?" he was famous for answering: "Good. Good as can be. I'm circling the drain is all."

The first time Daniel met Robert Heppler, he was in an intense discussion with another resident. The issue was whether you wanted to live your life over, mistakes and all, if given the chance, even if you made the same mistakes. The other man was all for more years regardless, but Heppler stood firm for the contrary view, insisting: "Once is more than enough, thank you!"

Heppler was in his room watching television. Daniel knocked at the half-open door before entering: "Mind if I—?"

"Be my guest," Heppler shrugged, barely casting a glance in Daniel's direction.

"Anything interesting?"

"See for yourself." Heppler pointed to the screen. An octopus was swimming away from the camera, eight arms stroking. "How'd'ya like that—running on all eight cylinders!" he said admiringly.

Suddenly a blast of blue-black ink covered the screen.

It was so strange: at first sight the creature seemed to be little more than a mouth and arms for stuffing that mouth. But each arm had a brain, according to the announcer, making nine brains in all. Two thousand fingers . . . if you counted the suckers on his arms as fingers. But now something new was drifting by: the shimmering silver blur coming into focus was never identified. Its fish-eye, perfectly round and blank as a button, was the same as the side-eye Heppler turned onto Daniel now.

What Daniel had to say could only be addressed to Heppler in profile since the room had only the one armchair, which Heppler presently occupied. He had no need for the visitor's chair that was assigned to each resident's room and had rejected it, leaving the bed as Daniel's only available perch. Administration had sent Daniel over to encourage Heppler to consider "final arrangements" and to make the case for "tradition," an unlikely assignment for someone Daniel's age and not known to be especially religious. He was once told that he was "more spiritual than religious." It sounded squishy and soft—shapeless. But he was not unchurched. His grandparents were staunch Methodists and saw to that, but since their passing, Daniel had been making his way on his own. This was part of his job; Daniel didn't judge.

"Why are we talking about this again?" Heppler began. "It's my decision, nobody else's. Nobody else has the right. I'm not 'in denial,' as certain people upstairs seem to think," he went on. "It's the opposite. And I'm not depressed, no more than anyone else here."

At issue was his refusal to plan—or allow anyone else to plan—his funeral. Heppler was eighty-eight; it wasn't unreasonable to bring up the subject now.

And the administration feared his example might be trending in the population at large. The staff psychologist had some stats to suggest Heppler was not the only one.

Long Day

Daniel had been given some talking points. He was willing to try them out. For instance: "Each of us has a story. Shame if it's lost—"

But Heppler wasn't having it: "My life is not a story—it's been one damn thing after another and sometimes all jumbled together. Call it anything you want—funeral, memorial, 'celebration of life,' life story—it's the same deal."

Daniel argued the usual, "It's not for you, but for those who remain."

There wasn't much conviction in his voice, though, for he was well aware that Heppler, like the rest of his "orphans," had no surviving people that anyone knew of, no one in particular remaining for him.

"Don't you want to let people here know who you are?"

"Who I *was*, you mean? Dead is dead. Why put a ruffle on it? No ceremony, no fuss."

Daniel was losing momentum, while Heppler seemed to grow even more energized. He was unshaven—prickly in more ways than one, bristling with sharp replies. But his color was good. No hurry: it looked like he would be hanging around for a while yet.

Daniel gave it one last try: "Isn't there anything you would like for us to do?" This time, Heppler paused.

"Well," he took a breath. "There is one thing I'd like *you* to do. Tell you what—" and before he knew exactly how it happened, Daniel had gotten himself involved, promising to deliver a small portion of Heppler's cremains to his favorite honky-tonk.

Honky-tonk? Heppler? Did Daniel hear the man right? Were honky-tonks still even a thing?

"Since you insist," Heppler added.

"And where exactly should I leave it, this ash?"

Heppler answered with a shrug: "Ashtray on the bar—spit bucket on the floor—don't make no difference to me." He shot Daniel another side-eye, a canny stare, calculating the effect he was having. Heppler wanted to shock, but Daniel was not about to give him the satisfaction. Still, he couldn't help feeling a little rattled.

It was a camping-out sort of life: Daniel told people he was "still sorting things," but in all these months he had only unpacked one fry pan and kettle and one place setting for dinner. He was still using one of the sealed cartons as a chair, another as his dining table--everything provisional. His grandparents' house remained on the market, unsold. He wouldn't take any action until a deal was closed. In the meantime, he was stalled if not stuck here.

Worn to a frazzle, all he could think of was bed. Would he be too tired to sleep? It had happened to him a number of times in the past month—*why?* His job was not physically demanding. There were no new stresses. And surely it helped to be among others who were grieving, to be sheltered in their circle of sorrow.

15

Another Spring

REALLY, THEY COULDN'T have asked for nicer weather. Gladys wouldn't be joining them at the bench today, though. She had had her hair done and didn't want to waste it, so she was going to church instead. The presence or absence of one person—especially in the case of Gladys, who never had much to say—shouldn't have made that much of a difference, but Daniel felt it right away. Her presence had tended to keep them a little more grounded, more tethered to common sense.

Wiktor had been reluctant to join the others on their bench during his first few weeks, but with so little other stimulation, he found himself with them, even participating to some extent.

Daniel was tired of searching for appropriate subjects for discussion. *Let someone else give it a try for once. But who? It would be a relief to relinquish control.*

When Daniel first started at Shady Rest, he brought the daily newspaper on the chance it might encourage conversation. It rarely did. From time to time, the staff debated the value of trying to keep people in their eighties and nineties current. There was no agreement on this. Some insisted on the "cognitive benefits" of keeping up with the wider world. Daniel had his doubts: *If it's a world they no longer have a part in...?*

Wiktor was obviously the most accomplished and qualified to manage a discussion, although with his retiring nature and the composition of the group, the attempt might be futile. Daniel often had a hard time finding innocent subjects of conversation, so if he were willing, let Wiktor give it a try.

He wasn't off to a promising start:

"Does anyone know how the Adam's apple got its name?"

Daniel was mildly curious, though he wasn't sure that anyone else was. Eli answered wordlessly, drawing a line across his neck with his forefinger. He wasn't entirely off. Right place, wrong gesture. If they had been playing charades, one would say that he was slashing his own throat.

"It looks like something in the throat he can't swallow or cough up." Maddie, at least, was listening. "And from the garden of Eden to now—it's still stuck there, to this day."

Maddie reminded them that the apple was from "the tree of the knowledge of good and evil," and they all knew where that came from.

"Yes, but why did they call it an 'apple'?" Daniel asked, trying to keep the conversation going.

Wiktor can't say for sure. Mistranslation from language to language was his best guess. "In Latin, 'apple' is 'malus' and 'evil' is 'malum.' You see?"

Not clear that any of them did see, but Maddie said admiringly, "I always wanted to study Latin...."

"I never went to charm school, myself," added Eli.

"Most assuredly not," Daniel heard Wiktor mutter under his breath.

Wiktor was talking mostly to himself now. Who was it that called human beings "featherless bipeds" and why? The reason seemed pretty obvious: to take them down a notch. Even Maddie had lost the thread of his argument, if that's what it was.

But feathers would be nice, Maddie imagined, thinking of their warmth and softness. She'd lost so much weight this past year and was nearly always cold, shorn of a necessary layer of cushioning. Wings she thought she could manage without (bones become brittle), but feathers would be nice.

Daniel thought they all seemed a little spaced-out. It was not only Wiktor's going on and on. All around them: skateboards and bikes were whizzing by. So much surplus energy available to burn! There would be few regrets in heading back inside.

Hoping to elevate the mood before they left, Daniel punched it up with a more cheerful topic: it was Freda Green. Wouldn't it be something if they all got to celebrate her hundredth birthday? Daniel didn't know how many of the residents had actually read the profile of Freda that he had written in the weekly schedule-bulletin. Few to none, he suspected. It had taken a whole lunch break for him to compose it. He credited Freda's positive outlook and her can-do attitude for her longevity. It was all a guess—a stretch—because what did he know? He had spoken to her maybe three times in as many months. She didn't look that old, but perhaps they failed to keep accurate birth records back in those days.

As soon as Daniel had gotten into the weeds on the subject of Freda, he had second thoughts about mentioning her at all. Why set people up for disappointment? How many people actually get to be centenarians? "The exception that proves the rule," was one of Wiktor's favorite sayings.

They gathered up their things.

The silence was palpable, the mood contagious.

Daniel felt it. Lately Maddie felt it. Eli always felt it.

Wiktor could not wave it away. Although discomfited by chatter, it was silence that weighed on him most heavily now. Moments like this. The silence thick in his ears.

Wiktor, last to enter the residence, thought he heard something following—a confusion of footsteps at his back. Imagining a patter of regrets echoing his own, Wiktor almost cried out: "Helen, is that you?"

But of course he knew better.

Turning down the long corridor past reception, Wiktor was drawn to an abrupt halt, one foot glued to the floor, the other pumping furiously up and down to no perceptible effect. All that anyone looking on could see would be the standstill.

Holding—four, five invisible beats, and released as mysteriously as he'd been taken.

There was a word for what was happening—*festinare*—a perfectly legitimate word with a solid Latin root for *hurrying*. He had been hurrying in place.

Also known as *stutter step*.

Festination was not unexpected with Parkinson's disease, as Wiktor was learning. It didn't feel like an ordinary stumble or stall, but rather two selves, two wills clashing in him at one and the same time. One to move, one to grind into earth, one to leave, one to stay, one to stiffen, one to soften . . . and still never move.

And now in the hallway, he was stuck. If there had been traffic, he would have caused a traffic jam. He needed to move his feet towards one of the chairs that lined the hall, but his feet ignored him. An empty wheelchair stood closest, but he wouldn't collapse into a wheelchair. *He could still choose his chair!* A few hard moments later, he sat. Was it possible that no one had noticed his silent panic? But there was still treachery ahead: he must be careful not to get too stiff to move again. A new worry was that Eli might happen by, offering unwelcome comradery. Luckily there were no chairs directly next to Wiktor. But without a book or any paper to read, there was no hiding the fact that he was sitting because he had to, not simply taking a break on a stroll down the dark hall.

Vanity, he recognized. When he first arrived, as a suggestion, Administration had left a cane in his room with four little feet so it could stand by itself. At attention. He didn't want that attention. He had been insulted by it and immediately hid it behind the chair in his room. It occurred to him that by never having even tried it, he might have passed the point of its usefulness. From walking to walker, too late for the cane.

Minutes later, he felt a small magnetic release of feet from linoleum, a moment of lightness, and knew he needed this window of respite to continue down the hall to his room.

It was not the first time this had happened.

Back in his bedroom, Wiktor paused at the closet mirror where a stranger stared back at him: no one he knew or cared to know. He touched the face in the glass and covered it with his hand.

Can it be that I am he?

Small irritations loomed large in the night, at the end of a day otherwise featureless. Eli, for instance. The way he could be counted on to derail any attempt at serious conversation. *Adult conversation—was that too much to expect?* The way he strutted and puffed out his chest whenever ladies were present. Sulking, when the spotlight shifted to someone else. Wiktor never expected, never *dreamt,* of spending his last days in the company of people like these.

It would be one of those nights: unable to sleep, tossing from this side to that side, or prone, flat on his back, or curled up in a fetal ball, head to knees, like something waiting to be born. The chattering of the clock on his bedside table would become too much for him—until he gave up and stuffed it into a drawer, where it would remain nested till morning, muffled by socks and undershirts. His relief would be real but temporary. Until he let go and started to drift and the faintest mothlike fluttering would return him with a jolt to this room, this too-narrow bed.

In the small hours, an owl on the hunt for prey would shatter the quiet, crying "Who? Who? Whoo?" alone in the night.

> The night nowhere near ending
> The long hours yet to get through
> The small hours the longest
> Yet these hours too would pass.

16

Planning the "Surprise"

DESPITE HEPPLER, memorials continued to be observed at Shady Rest. And, in the normal course of events, birthdays still outnumbered funerals by a wide margin. Years ago, someone had started calling birthday parties "surprises." There were people who thought that was clever and others who thought it was a lame joke. Is it still a surprise if it was announced on the bulletin board and in the newsletter, or was the surprise to have lived another year? Either way, Freda Green's "surprise" birthday was the next big event on the horizon. And it was coming right up.

Daniel was assigned to the committee responsible for "planning the surprise." Since no one in this group could claim any previous experience with birthdays for hundred-year-olds, they turned to the internet for tips. Their list was now making the rounds of the general staff for further suggestions.

It was mostly common sense.

Planning the "Surprise"

Here is what the list looked like so far:

1. Go over names of invitees with family members.
2. Review list of names a second time to make sure close relatives are not forgotten, addresses are current, etc.
3. NO GIFTS! To be spelled out in no uncertain terms. This is not a time for accumulation.
4. Starting and ending time for the party to be spelled out and strictly enforced.
5. No surprises. Surprises can be fatal.
6. Catering. Avoid spicy and acidic foods. Cake, casseroles, and small "tea sandwiches" best. Tea and fruit punch (non-alcoholic). Recipes invited from residents and staff.
7. Create a memory table (remember "This Is Your Life" on TV?). Including weddings and baptisms, ancestors' history (for example: first settlers to break the sod in Deaf Smith County). Unframed photos on bulletin board. Extra bulletin board for news clips about birthday girl, telegrams, etc.
8. Invite Senior Citizen band to lead brief singing of favorites from the good old days.
9. Decorations: Festive tablecloths, banners, and ceiling swirls.
10. No confetti! Slipping hazard.

11. Flowers: Limit floral displays for a number of reasons: allergies, breathing difficulties, reminder of funerals.
12. Activities for children. Children should not be underfoot. A separate play area, if it can be arranged, is recommended. Babies can be presented for picture-taking in a (brief) group photo. Supervision absolutely necessary.
13. Balloons (in moderation).
14. Hundredth birthday sash for honoree?
15. Names for tables. Place-holder seating cards.
16. Greetings. Toasts. Recollections. Should be few. And brief—2 to 3 minutes max.
17. Transportation arrangements.
18. Clean up volunteers.
19. Medical backup.

There would be no senior citizen band, no seating cards, and they knew they could never pull together a "memory table," but they would make every effort to apply the other suggestions.

What everyone wanted to know and would never ask aloud: *whether it was worthwhile, living so long.*

Sunny followed Daniel outside the door of the conference room.

Planning the "Surprise"

"Got a minute?" she caught up to him.

"Take five."

"Want to sit?"

"Weren't we sitting a minute ago?"

"Well, let's find a quiet spot."

They found a corner away from the others.

"So—what's up?"

"About Eli...."

"What about him?"

"They want him to come to us. Soon as a room's available."

"Who's 'us'? The Memory Unit? Does he know?"

"He's gotta suspect it. *Sheesh!* He's displaying all the signs."

"Because of the bathroom issue?"

"'Bathroom issue?' He's been exposing himself! Can't keep his hands off his zipper."

"Might be a bladder issue," Daniel said. "It's a worry with him—making it in time."

Sunny couldn't make up her mind whether Daniel was an old soul, or a child, or dim, or simply out of it—too long protected from life, too sheltered to know about the world. No telling about his future, inside or outside these gates.

It's true that he had a way with these people—a talent, if there were such a thing. She imagined that he would never leave this place.

He should be with people his own age. He was too young to be surrounded by the elderly all day. She remembered that he had grown up in the care of his grandparents and then as the sole caretaker for his grandfather. She didn't know of any hobbies or interests, friends or girlfriends.

It wasn't that Daniel was lazy. It was something else. If he were her son, she would want more for him.

In the following days, by asking and poking around (snooping, really), Daniel learned a few things about Eli that he had not known before—or had known, but not fully appreciated.

For one: the fact that he was born and raised in Happy, Texas—known as "The Town Without A Frown," also "The Town Without a Cavity" (due to the natural fluoride in the water, which turns teeth brown). That might have explained his nervous half-smile. About Happy: the town had started out called Scratch, due to its unpromising future, dry and meager. In a spirit of optimism, the name changed to Big Hat (Eli often recalled his marching band days at Big Hat High) when the first oil field was found. Big Hat became Happy only recently in a marketing strategy to encourage oil prospecting.

More facts about Eli: he was married twice. Divorced first, then widowed. A checkered career: accountant, farm auditor, auctioneer, antique restorer.

Planning the "Surprise"

He'd once been known to have extraordinary memory for detail. There'd been complaints that he seemed to think of himself as "a ladies' man," More than a few women here were put off by him.

Daniel noticed that the ratio of men to women here was roughly one to three. The gentle ladies, it seemed, were wearing out their menfolk at an alarming rate.

17

Movie Night

MOST SATURDAY NIGHTS they gathered in the common room to watch a movie selected by a small committee of "trustworthy" residents. The stories chosen tended to the tried and true. No nudity or foul language, unswervingly upbeat, with the good guys guaranteed to come out on top.

Recruiting staff members to supervise this activity wasn't as easy as it might sound, competing with family time or date night for the younger crowd. Daniel had no other commitments and thought he could use the overtime. The other staffer helping out—Joaquin—was working to pay off his student loan. Neither of them had any interest in these movies (which Joaquin dismissed as meant for kids).

The movie went like this: once upon a time two dogs, who had been neighbors for years, grew up and fell in love. They were named Buster and Betty and dubbed by once-famous American voices. Buster was a

Movie Night

boxer and Betty a mix—part poodle, part Corgi. They weren't the best-looking couple on the block, but looks didn't hold that much sway to dogs: sniffing and licking were more reliable and nose to crotch was the sweetest.

So Buster and Betty decided to become matchmakers for their humans. Agreeing to get their leashes entangled as a first step in what they thought of as a courtship dance for all four. It created an awful snarl and a knot they couldn't undo.

Suddenly—mysteriously—the room was flooded with light, and attention shifted from events on screen to Eli crumpled in his chair. Betty was returning from a beauty appointment at the groomer's and Buster was playfully biting her new bows and whispering sweet nothings in her ear. Eli's yipping and yapping were mistaken for one of the dogs barking at first.

But not for long.

"*Hup...Hup!*"

The yaps were hiccups. Eli's.

Water was offered; it didn't help. Remedies were called out: breathing into an empty bag, holding his breath, pulling his tongue, a lick of something sweet. Lint-covered cough drops were proffered from pockets.

The hiccups persisted—yelps in even triplets. So evenly spaced that they seemed deliberate and in fact someone muttered: "I think he's doing it on purpose," prompting someone else to counter: "On purpose? What could the purpose be?"

"If he doesn't like the movie, why spoil it for everyone else?"

Time to re-boot. Daniel suggested that Joaquin resume the movie while he and Eli stepped outside and waited a bit in the hallway until the attack subsided on its own. He could always page the night nurse on duty if it came to that.

"Let's give it a few more minutes," Daniel urged. "Then if you want to go back we'll go back. Or not. The others seem to be enjoying the film."

"Such shit! All that wagging and winking." Daniel did not dispute his judgment. At this moment, Eli did not sound much like a dementia patient.

"You don't have to stay and watch," Daniel reminded him. "No one's forcing you."

Eli yapped—twice.

"Maybe better if we sit for a bit and try not to talk," Daniel suggested.

Daniel had read about patients exhausted from hiccups going on whole days and nights, needing to be hospitalized and sedated—some even dying! Supposedly, fear alone could cause hiccups. Had someone already informed Eli that he was going to be moved to the Memory Unit? Could that be what this was about? Best not to over-think it. It was only hiccups so far. It seemed safe to assume that the group was carrying on inside and that they were not missed.

"What next?" Daniel asked after the hiccups subsided. "I've got to go back pretty soon, but I can see you to your room." He was anxious to get Eli into his room and out of his pants before anyone noticed that he had wet them.

"No need! No need!" Eli cried out in reply, springing to his feet and starting to wander off in the wrong direction.

Back in his room, Daniel helped Eli change into dry pajamas and settle in his recliner. Eli wasn't ready for bed and confessed to Daniel that he hadn't been comfortable sleeping in his bed for months now. At the moment he was free of hiccups and seemed sufficiently lucid to be left on his own. There was that small matter of his starting out in the wrong direction for his room, but that could happen to anyone at any time.

After he paged the nurse on duty to keep tabs on the situation, Daniel returned to the common room to find Joaquin folding chairs, his audience dispersed.

"We survived," Joaquin reported.

"To the end?

"To the very end. The very happy ending."

Falling asleep, Eli's head had twisted, and now a rude tongue was licking his cheek, folding and lapping in waves. It was the dog's kiss . . . that ridiculous movie. The wetness crept, touching the rim of his ear.

His mouth filled with darkness.

It was a nosebleed coming on.

It wasn't until morning that Daniel heard about Eli's nosebleed and was able to pick up the details—how Eli had treated the bleed on his own, packing his nostrils with toilet paper before letting any of the staff know. The nurse on duty pronounced his condition "not serious." All the doctor who reviewed the report would say was: "Monitor regularly. Apparently, the patient had a busy night—a cascade of minor mishaps."

Later in the day, when Daniel looked in on him, he found Eli arguing in his sleep, protesting to the air. "I won't! I won't go!"

"Won't go *where*?" Daniel pressed, but got no reply.

Someone must have spilled the beans about his scheduled move to Memory Care. Someone always does, despite HIPAA privacy protections. Daniel had planned to break the news to Eli himself, slowly and tactfully, at the right time and place.

18

The Thirsty Thistle

AS IT HAPPENED, Heppler passed "peacefully, in his sleep" (as they say) not long after the conversation about his ashes.

His worldly goods, such as they were, had been donated to one or another worthy charity. As for his cremains, the bulk were taken care of. *Best not to dwell on this.* The portion set aside for Daniel was only a fraction of the total—what did one call it?—output? Residue? The standard office supply envelope was not imposing or mysterious in any way, but it haunted him. Aside from it having been hand-delivered by the nurse in charge of Heppler's ward, Daniel knew next to nothing.

He poked around inside the manila envelope deeply enough to find the still-smaller bag, an ordinary plastic baggie. It was filled with what looked like sand, grayish sand and gravel.

A single Post-It note had been attached: Two words. *You promised*. No name, nothing.

Daniel now understood that Heppler had considered it to be a real promise.

He tucked the envelope away in a kitchen drawer, trying to forget where he put it. He tried moving it from drawer to drawer, as if that could domesticate it. He always pushed it to the back, so as not to see it right away. But it was always on his mind, even when he was unaware of it.

The day came when Daniel ran out of excuses not to go. Despite thinking he didn't remember where the packet was, a sixth sense took him exactly to it.

He placed the packet on the passenger seat beside him and caught himself turning to it more than once to argue: *Why am I doing this? Who would know—or care—if I never did it?* After the handing over, the office had made it clear that no one there had an interest in hearing more about it.

So who's to know? Why bother? Get rid of it!

But the answer came back always the same: *Because you promised.*

Daniel had lived in Brewster his entire life but never ventured out to this particular stretch of boulevard before. The blight affecting the entire north side of town was undeniable here. The new interstate built half a mile to the south was to blame.

The Thirsty Thistle

What remained were vacant lots for sale, set between squat cinder-block structures, most of them without name or clue as to what went on inside. Those that could be identified were predictably low-end enterprises: Doug's Ding 'n Dent auto repair, scrap metal resale, fast food, car wash, saloon. A Gentlemen's Club, boarded up, deep in weeds. Not far from this: The Thirsty Thistle —still *standing*.

So, here goes.

At the bar, he hesitated over the brand. *Which should it be—Lone Star or Pearl?*

Don't overthink this.

He decided on the obvious: *Lone Star it would be.* He slung back a few chugs right away, trying to feel less conspicuous. It was even more embarrassing to feel that way when hardly anyone else seemed to be around.

Meanwhile, the little baggie of ash smoldered in his pocket.

It was before Happy Hour, and there was nothing much doing. He could have waited until the parking lot filled up, but he was there now and primed, as much as he would ever be.

The light, what little there was of it, was garish: harsh neon relieved by pockets of gloom. He made his way along the edge of the scuffed bar where a lone couple—not young—was slow-walking and swaying to a recorded song. *Could that really be "Waltzing Across Texas With You in My Arms?"*—a fan-favorite at Shady Rest.

Daniel's heart was beating so loudly that he suspected others could hear it, despite the jukebox playing. A live senior citizen band occupied a table by the stage. The musicians seemed to be resting, idly strumming and scatting while they waited.

Daniel noticed that there was only one ashtray on the length of the bar, and it was already full. No sign of a cuspidor, either—should he try the Gents? Not for the first time it occurred to him that he could "forget" the packet in the men's room and be done with it.

He cleared his throat three times. "Still thirsty?" the barman asked, squinting at Daniel's nearly full beer.

How to begin?

Daniel must either explain why he was there or simply go home. Even now, it wasn't too late to consider turning on his heels and leaving the packet for others to deal with—but for the thought of the bartender calling after him: *"Forgot something?"* What then?

"Looking for somebody?" he asked, suspiciously.

"Some *thing*," Daniel clarified. Which of course clarified nothing, and Daniel decided then and there that the only way to be done with this was to tell the man.

Solemnly, Daniel handed the packet over. The bartender lifted it up to the light. "You messing with me?" he asked. "Better not be." Gently, he shook the thing, uncovering white specks and splinters—unburnt bone—in the grayish mix.

Daniel assured him: this was not his idea of a joke. For the first time he spoke Heppler's name, his full name—no reason not to. The bartender introduced himself as Joe. "Just your average Joe."

Given a moment to think it over, Joe admitted that maybe Heppler's request wasn't that far out. To be honest, he felt pretty much the same way about funerals: "Less said, the better."

Even so, he couldn't recall a customer, certainly not a regular matching Heppler's age and description, hanging out at The Thistle. "Course none of us getting any younger—but no one *that* far gone."

Daniel had no idea how many years might have lapsed since Heppler's last visit. He hadn't taken the matter seriously enough to press for more details at the time.

"One of the old timers might of knowed." Joe hollered over to the musician's corner: "Leroy! Haul your lazy ass over here."

Leroy limped over. He was quite a sight: long gray hair straggling out from under a battered Stetson, gold stud in one ear. Part stage Western with fancy lizard boots, belt fastened with a buckle the size of a saucer, advertising the very beer Daniel was pretending to drink.

Daniel did his best to explain. Leroy held out his hands to receive the packet, regarded it solemnly.

"Jeez ... *is this all?*"

Joe piped up, "Yeah, where's the rest of him?"

Leroy put the packet up to his ear and started humming. "I'm getting this tune in my head: hmm, hmm, mmm, hmm ... like a lonesome cowpoke song. I know the feeling. You know the feeling. *'Lost my saddle in . . . wherever, broke my leg in San Antone'* . . . however the hell that goes. I know the feeling! Might write a song about it myself."

"Awesome," Joe chorused.

"Actually," Daniel started, then checked himself.

Actually, Heppler worked at a desk job all his life. In an office.

But, shush, not another word! Daniel turned on his heel and scrammed, leaving the two of them hard at it, heads bowed over the little packet he'd handed them, not once looking up.

As soon as he was out the door, he remembered that he left his beer on the counter. But no longer needing pretext or prop and having delivered on the main thing, a promise kept, he was content to leave that behind as well.

Let it ride.

It had all turned out so much better than Daniel had expected—so why this lingering unease? Yes, he'd kept his promise, he delivered the ashes. He made it possible for Heppler to escape the "fuss" of the usual funeral, but he'd not prevented the placing of a "ruffle" around death (a memorial by any other name). Apparently even Heppler could not leave without draping himself in some small legend or story.

Daniel had discharged an obligation but learned nothing, really. What was this about, anyway? Was it for people to have "a tale to tell" about Bob Heppler after his death, making him more of a character than he actually was? Heppler was known for thumbing his nose at everything others considered solemn or sacred. Was it the completion of a long-ago dare—a way of having the last word? Or had Heppler been messing with Daniel all along? So many questions left unanswered. Unasked. Unanswered because unasked.

Even with his grandparents day after day, Daniel understood that there was much he would never know.

As it turned out, though, Heppler wasn't that easily shed.

Twice on the way back, Daniel turned to the empty space on the passenger seat beside him, and asked: "How we doing?" The empty space remained an empty space; it did not answer, it did not radiate. And then, because Daniel wasn't entirely at peace with the mission accomplished: "I hope you're satisfied. You ought to be."

19

Generations

THE DAY COULD HAVE been salvaged. Peter, Freda's youngest grandson, persisted in hoping that it might yet turn out to be a joyous occasion. It was entirely up to Freda.

In the meantime, the family had to wait outside Freda's room while someone helped her get dressed. The baby they had schlepped across three state lines to introduce to her started to fret. From inside the room, protestations could be heard. But at last Freda emerged, walker first, ready to present herself. She wore a blue jumper over a bright floral orange and purple dress. More colors than necessary. Her hair, even now not completely white, rose like a thin cloud cover over her freckled scalp.

Unfortunately for the visitors, this was shaping up to be one of Freda's silent days. "Don't let her fool you," the aide explained. "Usually she has plenty to say. She can be quite mouthy, in fact. She knew perfectly well that you were coming today."

Peter approached to kiss her papery cheek. "We've brought your youngest," he said. But Freda's gaze drifted.

"It's a girl. She's so bundled up it's hard to tell! But at her age, they all look pretty much alike." Confronted with Freda's silence, he continued chattering nervously. "I remember Dad telling me that they all look like Winston Churchill at the start."

The baby was named Hannah, after Peter's mother. Freda repeated the name, "Hannah." She seemed to recognize the name: Hannah had been her daughter, years gone by now. Baby's mother was then introduced. Did it register?

Peter was intent on memorializing this moment, in any case. With his wife at the camera, he positioned the baby by Freda's arm, to make it look like Freda might have actually been holding the child.

"Lift your head," his wife urged, "I can't make out your faces. Smile, everybody. Say 'cheese!'"

Baby yelped, protesting; she would have none of it.

Freda's gaze stretched far past the baby, beyond the family huddle, her crafty lizard eyes trained on the comings and goings at the end of the hall, as if they were the only items of conceivable interest. No wonder the baby screwed up her face, balled her fists, and made her feelings known. When Freda noticed the baby, and their eyes met, it was without curiosity or interest. The bottle was offered—slapped away—but the pacifier was accepted; it would do. For how long? For now. Do not ask beyond the Now. With baby's mouth plugged, taking pictures would have to wait, though.

Suddenly Freda perked up. There was some new commotion in the hallway. She released the handbrakes on her rolling walker.

"Mustn't miss her Bingo," the aide explained, as a parade of wheelchairs, walkers, and canes passed. That's where everybody was heading.

They were short-staffed again, and Daniel was summoned to officiate at Bingo: to spin the cage and shout out the numbers. Also—he hoped it wouldn't be necessary—to handle any conflicts that might come up.

Rushing down the corridor between the main building and the Memory Unit, he was puzzled by the uneven progress of the old man walking ahead of him. When the man came to a full stop to rest, leaning on his cane, Daniel recognized him as one of the newer patients and probably lost.

Daniel didn't mind slowing down to find out what the problem was—no point in hurrying. Not only was Bingo excruciatingly boring, it was also a bit insulting, assigning a paid staff-member to oversee something an untrained volunteer could easily manage.

"Are you lost? Heading to Bingo?" Daniel offered.

Generations

"It's confusing—hard to get the hang of," Daniel added. "All the halls look the same."

These words seemed to bring reassurance; the stranger repeated "they all look alike," as they moved along together at an even pace.

Maybe it was the bubbles rising in chains like silvery beads on a string, or the toy castle, or the submerged church with its red and gilt onion-shaped domes, or the fish themselves gliding to and fro in the fish tank, making a sort of wink in the water with each pass—whatever it was, baby smiled and burbled with delight. Now there was a problem with getting her to move on. They were causing a traffic jam in the hall.

Inside, folding chairs and tables were still being set up for Bingo. They were behind schedule.

Once a week, it had been the custom to invite a few "higher-functioning" patients from the Memory Unit to join the general population at Bingo. A special table was set up for them and a special aide assigned.

Freda, forgetting her visitors, passed the big table meant for residents who had guests. She squeezed into the table set aside for the Memory Unit patients. No room for Peter and his family, so they stood awkwardly behind her. One of the patients was stooping low, her nose only an inch or two from her bingo card. She was going blind and making sure that it was the same card, the aide explained. She always got the same card. Yes, she had some memory issues, but not with that card, she had memorized all the numbers and letters on it and never missed a beat.

"Have the rules changed?" someone called out. The question was routine, apparently; no one answered, and it was not asked again.

Baby, for her part, was on her best behavior. Her eyes rolled back, exposing a ring of white. She was swooning into sleep. Peter pulled on the pacifier, testing, and was answered with mute but powerful suction. "She's corked," he said. "Plugged, for now." His wife didn't like his attitude, didn't think it was funny. Baby's head wagged, keeping rhythm with the up and down movement of her pacifier.

At the front, Daniel took over. He gave the cage a few preliminary spins and flicked the microphone to test it. "Hello, everybody." He introduced himself, asked if they were ready to play, and received a few throat-clearing noises in reply. If he had more of a stage personality, or had made even a small effort, he might have gotten more of a response, but there was no point getting good at this, he reminded himself.

Without fanfare, he began. They used the caps from milk bottles as chips—blue from skim for ordinary numbers, red from whole milk for winning combinations. At the end, the reds would be counted and candies awarded—subject, of course, to individual dietary restrictions.

The aide at Freda's table produced a giant, blunt-tipped, knitting needle from the supply closet. She used it to point out the numbers on the patients' cards as they were called out. In the case of the woman seated across from her, who had been dipping down fussing with something on her lap and had covered her card with pretzels, her tapping sent a clear signal to cease and desist.

Then Daniel's microphone misfired. There was a big blurt of sound. Startled awake, baby began fretting again. Her mother gestured to Peter that they'd be out in the hall—taking a short walk, a breather, while he was tied up.

Down the hall, mother and baby approached the beauty shop. Except for the beauty operator and a single customer (a tiny woman about to disappear under a plastic styling cape), the place looked deserted. At the sight of this doll-sized woman, her head helmeted in bright pink rollers, smiling and beckoning to her, baby stretched out both hands and strained to free herself from her mother's grasp.

The doll woman waved and beckoned them both inside with her pink fingernails. Baby cooed with delight—the woman cooed right back, and they went on this way, a duet, back and forth—for longer than anyone might think possible. The beauty operator swiveled the chair around so baby could be brought in closer, the smiles and coos continued, all sweetness and light. But of course it couldn't last and ended with baby seizing her two front rollers, and pulling, the beauty operator shouting, and the old woman crumpled in tears.

Meanwhile, back in the game room, Freda had been fully occupied. She had won a game, earning a piece of chocolate. Since she wasn't under dietary restriction, she'd be able to enjoy her prize, but only after she'd eaten her supper.

"We'll keep it safe for you," the aide promised.

"Wonder why they call Hershey Kisses 'kisses'?" someone asked.

No one answered. They were too busy trying to file out in orderly fashion, avoiding collisions. Freda, self-propelled, had skillfully maneuvered her rolling walker, using it as a wedge, and managed to position herself near the head of the line. Peter struggled to keep up with her.

"It's no use," the aide said. "Believe me, I know. She's headed for the dining hall—she won't let anything stand in her way. Sure got an appetite, even now at 99. Catch up with her once she's situated."

Freda was already seated at her preferred table, scurrying distance from the deserts. A dish-towel bib had been set out for her, and she was busy tying it around her neck, when her family found her and joined her at her table. It was not yet 4:30. Serving began at 5:00.

Peter was determined now. "This is your youngest!" he announced too loudly. "Grandma Freda, Hannah. I want you two to get to know each other. We drove across three state lines for you to be able to meet.

We won't be able to make your hundredth birthday party, though we'd love to be there."

Peter lifted baby high enough so they could meet eye to eye.

But this effort was worse than useless. The tension in her father's arms must have communicated itself to baby, who started bellowing at the top of her lungs. Freda reached for her spoon and waved it menacingly over the tiny thrashing fists.

There were good intentions here—the best of intentions, for sure. Freda might or might not remember. Hannah surely would not.

Now the mother and father were stooped over the struggling infant, trying to soothe her. She pushed everything away—even her favorite pacifier, the pink one with the smiley face. Nothing seemed to work. Her father tried to amuse her by biting the pacifier himself and at the same time turning up the corners of his lips in an exaggerated smile, hoping—it's a game they played—she'd reach out to tug it free and stuff it, with redoubled appetite, into her own mouth. If only she'd quit bawling.

The pictures would have to be forgotten now.

Baby was plenty cranky now, with cause; she'd been completely thrown off schedule. Freda's indifference had nothing to do with disappointment; it wasn't a judgment on baby, she'd do fine. Why then did her parents, taking their leave, sound apologetic?

Had the visit been worth it? Later, Peter insisted that baby did smile, once, at the beginning.

Unfortunately, they hadn't caught that moment on camera; they hadn't been expecting it and missed it. They had tried: they made the effort, they remembered, they at least showed they cared. And wasn't that enough?

20

Foyer

MOST AFTERNOONS, ELI had taken to posting himself in the foyer ("where the action is") near the reception desk where he served as a one-man welcoming committee to everyone coming through the front door. From this post, he had earned a reputation as the Go-To for the latest in-house news and gossip. He was the first resident to learn about the new Director of Public Relations and the proposed expansion of the Memory Care Unit.

He seemed to be energized by all the coming and going—part of the "stream of life" the ads for senior living had promised.

He nearly always had something to say. The empty question: "How are things?" might have prompted the reply: "Good—but not with me." And might lead on from there. He had been seen more than once giving a push to someone in a wheelchair who might not have asked for it.

Solace, the regular receptionist, tried to establish a few guidelines by making Eli aware of those habits of his which made other people nervous. Like when he jingled pocket change when speaking. And when he tried to clean his ear with a matchstick or a key.

Otherwise, as long as Eli remained polite, calm, fly zipped, and his comments caused no scandal, he was welcome to continue as a volunteer greeter in the reception area.

One last thing: absolutely no prowling the reception area or loitering in the lobby after visiting hours.

How long Eli would be able to hold on was anyone's guess. They were waiting for the room to become available in the Memory Unit. They expected it would be a matter of days—any day now. Though still physically strong, only last week Eli had taken a fall outside the dining room. No broken bones, fortunately, but for minutes afterwards he did not know where or who he was.

Other residents—who must have noticed—said nothing. Except for Maddie, who drew Daniel aside to ask: "Is it serious?"

"It sort of is." Daniel said, finding it impossible to lie to Maddie.

III

21

Blank Screen

THIS WAS THE DAY that Eli was scheduled to move to the Memory Care Unit, but the patient they assumed would be vacating the room was not inclined to die yet, so they had to wait. No other room was available.

Daniel was worried about how Eli was taking the news. More concerned than worried, he imagined that the postponement might be as difficult for Eli to get through as the actual move. Also, the sight of a familiar face might give him a boost. Finding the door to his room ajar, Daniel poked his head in. No sign of Eli: it looked like he'd left in a hurry.

Long Johns and winter clothes were gathered on one end of the bed, summer clothes on the opposite corner. A heap of unfolded underwear lay between them, and atop the heap was an eagle feather with faded ribbons dangling. A trophy, Daniel imagined, from that famous Powwow years back in Shawnee.

The old-timers no longer spoke of it, but Eli had mentioned more than once that he had been there. Maybe he really had. It had been a Powwow for peace, starting out so promisingly, and ending so badly, in an ordinary barroom brawl.

He could think of only a few other places Eli might have been; it shouldn't be hard to find him.

The common room was located midway between Reception and the Memory Care Unit. Beside the door was the large locator map that proclaimed, "You Are Here," with its red arrow. You couldn't miss it. Yes, this is where Eli would be. Daniel turned in.

But Eli wasn't there.

Daniel had to sit down for a minute. He had been hurrying; his heart was beating fast. He fumbled for a chair, closed his eyes.

When he opened his eyes next, the light had changed. It was brighter now, but still not transparent or clear. Milky, maybe. More time than seemed possible must have elapsed.

He had lost all sense of following. Hadn't he been looking for Eli? Yes, that was it. Maybe he could find him later at dinner. No hurry. But the double doors were heavy, and when he reached to push them open, they snapped-to and locked shut. Daniel would have to wait to be released. He was curiously calm.

You are HERE, he reminded himself.

He knew where he was.

IV

22

Cake

SEAWATER EVERYWHERE. . . . Tipped back in his reclining chair, rocked by the breaking wave, he raced the swirling foam to shore.

It was one of those full-bladder dreams, and Eli was almost too late.

Back to his chair. He tried stretching out again to salvage whatever sleep remained. His one window floated up out of the blackness. He slept through first light.

Something special happening today, he recalled. *He can't hardly wait.*

What was the name of this feeling?

"Look who's here!" an aide prompted Freda.

Someone was standing and waving down the hall.

"Who is it?"

"You tell me."

Freda, in a transport chair, dropped her feet and dragged them, making it clear to the aide pushing her that, if she wanted to get closer, she'd pick up her feet.

"Why is that old man waving at us, is he moving in?"

"That 'old man' is your son."

"Can't be!"

"But it is. He's not moving in, that's an oxygen tank, not a suitcase. He came for your party."

"Take me back in, I'm not ready."

"This is your second costume change, Freda."

"Another!" she demanded, and tried to shuffle herself back to her room.

Once again, Amy the reporter had promised to write a story for the local paper. A Centennial Birthday, after all! And a local television news station had hinted that a team might be dropping in.

Anticipating interviews to come, The Weather Sisters had tried to coach Freda on the questions she should expect. People were sure to ask her what her secret was for living such a long life: special foods she'd recommend, habits, healthy attitudes, activities, games—that sort of thing. Naming Dr. Pepper as her favorite drink was fine but promoting the stronger stuff she really favors was not—not with so many Baptists around.

"Bingo!" Freda added.

"Absolutely," Sunny concurred. "Keep that ol' brain ticking."

"Touch your toes," said Freda.

"But not while standing," Misty cautioned, "only when sitting in a chair."

"Mind your own business," said Freda.

"Not nice," Sunny put in. "Is that what you're gonna say to the TV people?"

"Take a bow," said Freda, already on her feet, "I'm done here."

As it turned out, they needn't have troubled: Freda refused to submit to another rehearsal, and the local television affiliate never bothered to show up or even call. Amy did call to beg off for her paper at the last minute. You couldn't blame her or anyone else: a Garth Brooks look-alike had been discovered hiding among everyday folk in the audience at the county music festival also going on now. Mistakenly called out as the real thing, the announcement started a small stampede.

You couldn't blame them for wanting to be where the action was.

Eli recognized Wiktor down the hall from his awkward gait. He was walking slowly, headed in the opposite direction. Maybe he didn't remember that it was Freda's birthday party. Eli murmured a faint "how do?" to the air dividing them, wanting to make sure Wiktor remembered the big event, but it was doubtful whether Wiktor heard him or was ignoring him.

Right on time! Birthday balloons! But why did Eli feel so uneasy? It's only that for a second it occurred to him that maybe the celebration was not for his birthday. But the important thing was confidence, not to hesitate or waver. So he headed for the front of the room, steering past the sugar-free table, craving something truly sweet. He was entitled.

With his shirt tail untucked, buttons fastened out of sequence, comb-over askew, he looked, as one of the staff said, "like an unmade bed." Out of character for the man they knew as Eli. And that wasn't the worst of it, for Eli seemed bent on squeezing himself in at the table of honor next to Freda, who rightfully claimed pride of place. No one was willing to make an issue of this; so, with minor adjustments, scooching over this way and that, tucking their elbows in to make sure that Freda's son had room to breathe, the other guests yielded space to accommodate the new arrangement.

Freda was certainly dolled up for the occasion. Her hair was puffed, topped by a silvery (aluminum foil) party crown. Her skin glowed, a picture of health, thanks to a smudge of blush on each cheek. And she was wearing her best Sunday dress, dark blue with a sparkling white lace collar, and new silver running shoes. Her birthday corsage, a white orchid, was taped to her wrist.

Cake

Before digging into the goodies, Freda was asked to lead the group in "returning thanks." At each table, heads dipped, hand sought out hand, a circle formed. At the table of honor, Maddie held tightly to Eli's hand, a gesture of support but also a warning: *no funny business*. She didn't trust him for a second.

Long pause, a hush, as they waited for Freda's blessing. Their expectations were so set that they did not hear what she actually said but only the usual invocation "Heavenly Father." Only what Daniel heard was distinctly different—unmistakable: "Here we go! To the door!"

Except for Eli squeezing in and the reporter's no-show, so far, things had gone mostly as planned. But then, without warning, Freda was on her feet. At first Daniel thought this might be the promised skit, a performance. He was unprepared when he realized it wasn't.

What in the world?

With a sudden swerve away from the table, Freda was on her way, showing what her new state-of-the-art rolling walker could do. Daniel tried to side-swipe her, missed, stumbled, grabbed a fistful of air, while Freda, expert navigator, swerved again, smacked the wall—ricocheted, teetered, recovered. Two deft corrections and she was in the straightaway, free and clear, racing for the door, the pink bottoms of her silver running shoes flashing rhythmically, pandemonium in her wake.

The surprise! Who would dream she could move so fast?

Freda's son looked as confused as any of the residents. Struggling to stand and follow, he fell back in place with a helpless gesture. Eli leaned towards the open door, but Maddie had him pinned, her hand over his hand. It wasn't the weight of her hand that stopped him, but how firmly, how carefully placed, as if to cover a stain.

"They're never coming back!" Eli wailed. "I know it!"

"We must let Freda go," Maddie explained. "This is *her* moment. And it's only a skit, they promised a skit—a surprise—so this must be it. Besides," she added, when Eli persisted in looking so sad, "I bet Daniel's almost caught up."

"Go, gal!" From a table close to the door, someone cheered. "Atta, girl! Go! Go, go, go!"

When Freda burst through the emergency exit door, Daniel was close on her heels, the alarm shrilling.

By the time the head nurse got to them, it was all over; Daniel had wrestled Freda to a standstill, she was visibly shaking and, as she recounted afterwards, "couldn't speak for laughing!"

What was so funny?

When Daniel came to a full stop, he pressed his hand to his chest, an old habit. The beat was racing, but strong—there was nothing wrong with his heart. *What if there never had been? (He wouldn't let himself*

Cake

think of those lost sports and friendships. He didn't want to be angry.)

"Come, let's have some cake!" They returned to shouts and applause.

Settling back at the table of honor, Freda was breathing heavily but grinning ear to ear, her foil crown askew, tilted over one eyebrow. One of the nurses squashed it slightly in recentering it and planting it securely.

Maddie gave Eli's hand an extra pat before releasing it. When the noise level subsided, he turned to her and said: "I'm going away, you know. Got to pack up and go."

Searching his face, Maddie saw that he was fully present for once. "Well," she answered, "You'll be right down the hall."

"Because I can't stay. Why? *Why* can't I stay?"

"But you're here. Now. For the time being."

"Time being," Eli pondered, but the words were mere puffs of air; he couldn't think what they meant.

Only a fraction of a moment's pause before the party was fully underway. Someone called out "How many *are* we?" and someone else counted and another took a tape measure to a late arriving fourth cake that had to be divided into perfectly equal portions to avoid bickering. They were almost entirely ready except for candles—what klutz forgot candles? Only one was really necessary, as they'd agreed, for only one of the cakes, because who's got breath for more?

But there must be *no fewer* than one candle.

The head nurse had scurried off to file an incident report, and at last they were singing "Happy Birthday to You," not forgetting the verse: "and many more." *More? Really?* Maddie had her doubts. *Have the extra years been worth it, Freda? Really?*

Sunny blew out the candle for Freda who admitted to being slightly winded, not from running but from laughing. The party was in full swing. They were singing, "*I wonder who's kissing her now, I wonder who's teaching her how,*" Eli's voice strong and melodic, remembering all the words, while plastic cups half-filled with lemonade were raised and paper plates passed around with slices of cake—a chocolate, two whites, all heavily frosted, and one impossibly pink, sugar-free.

Laughter washed over them, swelling from whispery to hoarse—almost gasping—almost weeping. Freda chose chocolate.

When yet another slice of cake (white with a blue rosette) was passed by him, Eli pushed away the one he'd been working on and reached out with both hands to receive the new portion. Eli hummed as he chewed, reminding himself to taste before he swallowed.

"Dementia, severe memory loss"—these labels had started to color all that Eli said and did. Such is the power of naming—of medical naming, in particular. Ordinarily Daniel would have welcomed the sight of Eli reaching for a second helping—evidence of an undiminished appetite for life—but now he questioned whether Eli really understood that it was a second helping, a repeat before he had finished the first, rather than the first slice for the first time.

Only later, hours after the party things had been packed away, was Maddie able to gather a coherent account of Freda's escapade.

Freda's little "skit" was meant to be a surprise, not a shock; a walk, not a run. She had rehearsed her celebration walk with one or another of The Weather Sisters all week. Chosen to accompany her for safety's sake, Sunny was supposed to be positioned next to Freda for an easy in and out. That was before Eli squeezed in between them. Daniel lost no time taking off in pursuit but wasn't quite quick enough to catch Freda before she burst through the emergency exit door, setting off the alarm and scaring residents and staff half to death.

Freda had promised Sunny never to touch that door. No one would have imagined that she could push it open by herself anyway.

Wiktor, having eventually come to terms with the four-pronged cane, paused in the hallway long enough to witness Freda and Daniel crashing through the outer door. He'd found the whole performance rather pathetic. What was no doubt intended as a celebration of—if not a bid for—freedom became a test of compliance. Yes, Freda was free to move—but also leashed. Free to the full extent of her chain and easily reeled back in.

23

Later

ELI CARRIED HIS PLATE from the party back to his room. Enough on it to do for supper. Early to bed and early to rise was his plan. Inspired by Freda's run for it—her almost breaking free. He told himself: *Tomorrow, my turn.*

Eight a.m.: getting through the hall was no problem. The maintenance crew for the morning was made up of temp workers hired to clean up Freda's celebration who did not recognize Eli as a patient. He jingled the coins in his pocket to sound like car keys, as he had noticed the real staff doing on their way out.

And amazingly, he passed. Eli simply slipped by them, leaving through the front door, unnoticed in plain sight.

But maybe not unnoticed for long. Better get a move on.

Outside, he moved swiftly at first, then slowed: the path ahead was slick, likely to be slippery.

He heard something.

"Who spoke?" There was no one around. It was too early.

But—*there it was again!*—the sprinklers were at it, nodding and dipping, their plumes ghostly in the early light. Whispering—about him?

What he needed was to sit and rest.

The bench was not too far off.

Someone seemed to have beaten him to it though. The bench was occupied: a man lay on his back sleeping, stretched out to his full length.

Moving towards the sleeper, Eli rehearsed what he would say: "Excuse me! This is where we meet. We're old—must sit down or fall down. There's four of us. It's hell getting old...." He could imagine how that would go over. Nevertheless, he moved towards the sleeper. Whether bench, grass, or pavement, he had to sit.

But when Eli reached the bench and touched actual wood, the young man was nowhere.

Gone, vanished without a trace, as if he never was.

Eli never caught a glimpse of his face. But now let Eli rest. *So many roads.* So many roads he'd been down; it tired him out just thinking about it.

He napped briefly.

He woke, unrefreshed and with a headache, the sun in his eyes, sun-blot everywhere he looked. There was some customer service hold-waiting music and words faint but unmistakable: "We're sorry; your call is important to us."

One thing he did know: he must get back in time if he wanted breakfast.

He wanted breakfast.

He was stepping off the curb before he realized that he was still outside the gate. Plenty of time, though, to cross the street before that sanitation truck came anywhere close. Time enough to beat the stoplight before he stooped to gather a few castoff coins gleaming against the asphalt. *Waste not, want not*, the words came to him—

24

Memorial

NO ONE GOT in trouble. The Public Relations specialist explained that it had been an issue of jurisdiction: a gap, an uncharted space which Eli had simply slipped through. He was still a part of the residence, which was considered Assisted Living, and as such was not yet bound by the rules and regulations of the Memory Care Unit.

A week from the day of Freda's party, they gathered for Eli's memorial service. Unsurprising that it should have been so well attended, for, like him or not, he certainly got around. Gladys said a few words. "Always the life of the party. Or trying to be," she began. She didn't of course say how much Eli irritated her. How hard it was to shake him.

He still seemed to be lurking everywhere. Maddie didn't say it, but lurking was the word for it. "He wasn't a big man, but he had a big personality," is what she came out with. "And a good singer. As I discovered last week. A really good voice, strong and melodic and, yes, he remembered all the words; he did have some deep down memories, remembered every hymn—carried along by the music as long as the music lasted."

Two other speakers. They said what people always say.

This much was true: He was friendly. He tried to be.

A real fire-cracker . . . his laughter was infectious. He lifted our spirits—sometimes.

Eli might have been anyone.

Wiktor, wandering the hall, paused at the doorway, lingering only long enough to determine that it was in fact Eli's enlarged photo-shopped face on the easel beside the lectern.

Much improved by death, in Wiktor's opinion. More hair, smile no longer hidden in the dense thicket of his moustache, as handsome a man as he imagined himself to be.

He had no intention of joining the group, but stalled for the moment on the threshold, just to look.

Masi, a new nurse from a country that most people there had never heard of, was about to shut the door but paused for Wiktor. "Come on in—if you're coming." She hadn't yet learned the proclivities of the residents, how Wiktor positioned himself always on the circumference of things.

Before turning away, he gave a nod, or perhaps the slightest of bows, towards Masi and the others. Gentlemanly, polite.

He tried to get going again, but his stutter-step had rigidified. Those who knew him before, upright and confident, were struck by the change. It was obvious that the cane was inadequate and unsafe. Anyone passing him in the hallway closely enough would have heard him whispering: "Pass ... pass ... pass ... move ... pass ... left foot long step ... long step long step." Nodding, lips moving, one could assume he was deep in prayer. But he'd been a prideful, never a prayerful man. In fact, he was asking permission, pardon, and release for presuming to move at all.

Recently, his mornings began with this litany:

> Instructions to the body:
> *Please cooperate today.*
> *If you would, I could—*
> *If you would, I would—*
> *If you could, I could—*
> *If I would—*

His condition had worsened—he was nicer now than before.

Inside, sitting down, Daniel reminded himself that his only assignment for the rest of the afternoon was to keep an eye on Freda. He sat on her left, guarding the aisle, waiting for mischief, which never materialized. Freda kept nodding off, all the starch leached out of her.

Sunny was the one who worried about Daniel. Now, from the corner of the room, she watched him. He seemed off-track. She knew Eli had touched Daniel, but she wasn't sure why. It was hard to believe that Eli might have reminded Daniel of his slow and steady grandfather. Eli was a show-boat of a man. That couldn't have been it. But who knows what a person gets and gives to another person? It would take a few months before Daniel understood not to get attached. There was really only one exit door for the residents; he would get used to it.

He was relieved not to have to speak. Relieved but not released. Instead, his thoughts returned again and again to the same questions and a few new worries. The Weather Sisters had picked up rumors of a new sickness going around, from China, a kind of flu never seen before; the elderly and their caregivers were particularly vulnerable. As far as he knew, it had not touched anyone here. Too far away—no one knew anyone from China. No need to borrow trouble.

No life without risk, inside or outside these walls.

Daniel had been surprised to learn that there were always a few residents who believed their lives from before were still waiting for them. They refused to give up their house keys. But this was not rehab. This would be their last home.

Looking around the room now, he didn't think many of these people wanted to leave. Most of them harbored no illusions. They wanted to stay. As long as they could. Where they were. Just stay. Be *safe*; that was enough for them.

Daniel didn't have to stay. He was too young to have to stay. He was staff; he could always leave. Granted, he would be forfeiting many perks: a subsidized apartment with its five-minute walk to work, health insurance, utilities, etcetera. Not to mention that the residents, especially his "orphans," might feel abandoned. Ultimately, he had to admit, the job was not so bad.

Lately, his worries clustered around the opposite concern: what if he never left? Daniel couldn't shake the feeling that the world expected him to want more.

On his way home, it occurred to him that he was passing the gate through which Eli had entered the stream of traffic. Had he rushed to join it in a blur of confusion? Or was it because he remembered something—that they were supposed to move him to the Memory Unit that day?

25

Dream

THAT NIGHT, MADDIE found herself back at Freda's party. Same party, same place, people she'd never met among the all-too familiar. A circle dance had begun. There went Freda and Gladys. Daniel joined them. Maddie knew it was a dream because there were no canes or walkers, no one shuffled or stumbled; she herself was moving unassisted with the ease and confidence she had lost years ago. There was the red-headed lady from the dining room singing out: "Dance, Dance! When you can't walk, it's the only way to go!"

And now Maddie was doubly sure it was a dream because Freda was banging away on an old piano, setting a tempo that was too fast, and there were no complaints, no collisions—and because Eli was calling the steps and the others following—he must have been making sense to them.

> Swing the lady off her feet
> Lift them all

Dream

You have the call—

There was plenty going on—stomping feet, swirling and flipping of skirts—a flirting of skirts. This was Eli's dance after all.

"Boys, bow to the ladies—" and the strange thing was that she—Maddie—was giving the words to him, dreaming Eli's dream for him.

> Ladies—curtsy if you can
> Do Si Do, then face to face,
> Hand over hand,
> Promenade and
> Allemande.
>
> Pass through
> Go Round
>
> Who's that coming?
> Could it be?
> My One and Only waiting for me?
> For me?
>
> Pass through
> Go Round

A shout from the dancers scattered them. It was Gladys crying out: "There's my husband, Ray! Ray, hon, I'm here! But who's that with you? I don't know her—" And, turning, she appealed to the others: "My husband's left me for that woman! Her hair's on fire!"

From the dim hallway to an open field bursting with light, the other dancers struggled to keep the beat set by Freda. The spaces between them uneven, they remained joined nevertheless, woven together for a moment, for that moment—whole. They were one, they were many: one body, many moving parts.

When Eli broke free, the circle was torn. Here the dream ended.

Maddie stirred, woke into herself. Alone. Apart. Still pitch black. *What time was it?* Long before daybreak, the first birds proclaimed it, light somehow seeping through the darkness all the while.

Maddie reached the handle of the walker she could not yet see but knew was there, standing by the side of her bed. The cane no longer sufficient, she had been told that she must think of the walker as her friend.

"Friend," she whispered, reaching out to touch it.

What a week it had been! Freda had given them all quite a scare. Her little pantomime seemed pure mischief at first, not at all amusing, yet thinking back now that it was safely over, Maddie saw the episode differently. There seemed to be method and message in it, a way of saying *I'm still here, still reaching—not done yet—*

But how many times has she been told she reads too much into things?

26

Another Spring

IN THE WEEKS AND months that followed, there were birthdays, memorials, petty meannesses, kindnesses, and everything in between.

When the Deputy Director fell ill with the mysterious new flu, there was talk of Daniel replacing him. Rather young for such a weighty job, but it was thought that youthful fortitude might be a bulwark against the new sickness. Also, Daniel was the only employee that had no complaints filed against him. A compromise was reached, and Daniel was promoted to Assistant Deputy Director, with a minor raise in salary, a private office (more of a coat closet with a desk), and a guarantee of two more years of subsidized housing on the property.

He felt protected by the flock. Last winter he had the idea that to encourage enthusiasm for breakfast: dessert should be on offer even in the morning. No problem for the kitchen staff as they merely recycled dinner's dessert. But when the Staff Nutritionist got wind of the sudden popularity of breakfast, she quashed it immediately. No one revealed that it had been Daniel's idea—a sure sign, he knew, of their warmth and support.

And the others?

It was said that Maddie "died in her sleep." But in truth, she had been found on the floor of her room, twisted in a position that suggested it had not been an entirely peaceful end. She had been well-liked and therefore was missed and mourned (in that order) and mentioned even into the next week.

In late September, Wiktor also died in his sleep. He succumbed to the virus, as would many others in the year to follow. Towards the end, he had been heard to sing or moan in what was assumed to be his native language but might have been gibberish. Daniel had hoped to be the one to interpret Wiktor's words or sounds, but one day in April, entering, he encountered a room steeped in silence. Daniel was the one who found Wiktor.

It was early morning, before the cleaning crew arrived in their hazmat suits. Astronauts. Who was the old surgeon in mask and gloves framed in Wiktor's mirror? That figure would be Daniel, unrecognizable to himself. Approaching the person—*himself*—he saw one large, smudged handprint on the glass, his face behind it. The print was ungloved; it must have been there a while. A starfish of a handprint, with an unnatural splay of fingers. Wiktor had once described some of Parkinson's symptoms to Daniel, and he remembered that this particular curvature of the fingers was called "swan's neck."

Could Daniel's gloved handprint match Wiktor's wobbly one? He pressed his palm to the glass and lined up his hand to match Wiktor's, finger to finger. But Daniel's fingers could not stretch as widely. Later, he imagined that Wiktor might have left the print for him as a parting handshake.

Things had changed since the reliable routines of the year before. Shady Rest would have been unrecognizable to Eli or Maddie. The looming and mysterious illness that had threatened for so long had finally landed, especially eager to consume the elderly. The virus thrived in the close atmosphere of Shady Rest, both in the residence and the Memory Care Unit. Stresses were compounded by the onslaught of sick patients arriving from local hospitals that had maxed out their rooms and services. It wasn't only Shady Rest: nursing homes all over the city had been pressed into service. Rolling hospital beds lined the halls that were accustomed to hosting two or three napping residents in wheelchairs. Gone the cheerful nurse's uniforms with bears and hearts. In their place a relentless cycle of disinfected hospital scrubs, green until they ran out and other colors rotated in. Administration was similarly uniformed, and Daniel was self-conscious that it might appear that he was pretending to be a doctor.

With masks on, everyone looked to be a stranger: friend or foe? Who to trust? The scene reminded him of old war movies he had watched with his grandfather, but this was different: not as dramatic as explosions or bloody soldiers on field stretchers. Ventilators made the only noise. As packed with people as it was, no one spoke, as though the virus itself were breathing and no one wanted to disturb it or make it angry. Visitors had been prohibited for a month or two now, and the Shady Rest residents had retreated into their rooms, unwilling to share air with the uninvited and contagious. The staff were testy, likely to crack at a moment's notice or a patient's sneeze (or worse) that accidentally landed on them. Shady Rest, a place accustomed to its residents "moving on," had never experienced so much moving on.

There was no quarter.

On the way to his office, Daniel noticed a tiny handprint on the glass of the fish tank. A baby? Gloveless? As he walked down the hallway, he saw more ungloved handprints. Didn't anyone else see it? As a strict advocate and enforcer of sanitary procedures, he would have to speak to Maintenance about this. Unless he was imagining it, dreaming it. How to know?

The day had been unsettling from the start, and the walk to his new office seemed longer than usual. When he arrived, he locked himself in. Double checked the lock. The room was so small, no room for more than a desk and an office chair. Daniel lay down beneath his desk, the only place he could stretch out. He removed the mask covering his mouth and nose and placed it over his eyes. Then he waited for his heart to slow down.

27

Birds on a Bench

ANOTHER SPRING and three new "orphans" gathered on the familiar bench. Counting Daniel, there were now four. Once again, he was the only one who had been orphaned in the literal sense.

Daniel found himself still looking for Maddie. Maddie, who was never late. He could almost see her in the distance, moving uncertainly towards the bench with her rolling walker.

But it was that new resident. What was her name? He had to do better remembering them.

Another spring and by now Daniel had unwrapped the moving blanket from his grandfather's easy chair. He had started unpacking boxes.

The year of Elora, Eli, Maddie, and Gladys had mellowed Daniel, and this sickness with its drama and desperation had aged him. He had become attached to the place, part of its heartbeat. More situated than perched now. There was good work to be done here.

A young couple jogging at a clip nearly swiped the new resident, the one Daniel thought might be Maddie. It made her wobble and struggle to regain her balance.

The couple didn't notice.

The soles of their sneakers slapped the pavement in unison. When the man slowed, the woman slowed.

"Why'd you stop?" The woman tugged at his arm. "What's there to see?"

A tree, a bench, birds, a bunch of birds—

"Nothing, nothing," he said, " just birds," pointing to the bench and picking up the pace.

Four featherless bipeds on a bench—

"Beat you to the gate!" She pulled in the lead.

"No way!" he said.

"We'll see about that!" she said.

They're off—heels flashing, picking up speed, glancing neither right nor left, but ever only ahead—

There they go—

This book was set in Adobe Caslon Pro, designed
by Carol Twombly and released in 1990. The typeface
is named after the British typefounder William
Caslon (1692–1766) and grew out of Twombly's study
of Caslon's specimen sheets produced between 1734
and 1770. Though Caslon began his career making
"exotic" typefaces—Hebrew, Arabic, and Coptic—his
Roman typeface became the standard for text printed
in English for most of the eighteenth century,
including the Declaration of Independence.

This book was designed by Shannon Carter,
Ian Creeger, and Gregory Wolfe. It was published
in hardcover, paperback, and electronic formats
by Slant Books, Seattle, Washington.

Cover photograph by Vasilica Ciocan via Unsplash.

www.ingramcontent.com/pod-product-compliance
Lightning Source LLC
LaVergne TN
LVHW092346130125
801209LV00033B/933